THE DEAF CAN SPEAK

THE DEAF **CAN** SPEAK

Pauline Shaw

faber and faber

LONDON · BOSTON

First published in 1985
by Faber and Faber Limited
3 Queen Square London WC1N 3AU

Filmset by Wilmaset
Printed in Great Britain by
Whitstable Litho Ltd Whitstable Kent
All rights reserved

© P. M. Shaw 1985

British Library Cataloguing in Publication Data

Shaw, Pauline
  The deaf can speak.
  1. Deaf
  I. Title
  362.4'2   HV2380
  ISBN 0–571–13424–6 ✓
        007 3084

To my family, friends and colleagues, without whose interest and support this book would never have been written, but above all, to Judith herself, whose courage and determination provided the inspiration

CONTENTS

Author's Preface   *page* 11

Glossary   13

Part One – Judith

1. The Perfect Specimen   17
2. Finding Out   21
3. One Year Old   25
4. A Day to Remember   29
5. Help from Abroad   32
6. One of the Family   36
7. Off to School   40
8. Four to Six   43
9. Can Julia Hear?   49
10. Growth in Speech and Language   54
11. Fitting in with Hearing Children   59
12. Widening Horizons   64
13. A Difficult Decision   69
14. Boarding School   73
15. Keeping in Touch   81
16. The Teenager   85
17. Growing Up   91
18. What Shall I Be?   98
19. The Undergraduate   105

Part Two – Understanding the Deaf

20. Transition   117
21. Understanding the Ear   119
22. Social Difficulties of the Deaf   124

23. How to Help the Deaf Child   127
24. Lip-reading   134
25. The Hearing Aid   137
26. Helping Your Child to Talk   143
27. Encouraging Memory   152
28. The Older Deaf Child   157
29. The Provision of Support for Parents   166
30. The Hearing Impaired Child in Mainstream Education   169
31. Children of Another Way   172

Useful Organisations   174

AUTHOR'S PREFACE

Deafness, and particularly profound deafness, with all the problems it creates, is seldom understood by the general public, and there is in all of us a tendency to shy away from what we do not fully understand. The barriers go up, and, to many, normal communication is deemed impossible.

When our daughter, Judith, was first diagnosed as profoundly deaf we suffered from the same sense of shock that other similarly placed families will appreciate. What on earth did it mean? And how could we cope? That we did cope, I trust this book will show. That great effort was demanded of us – and of her – is incontrovertible, but that the end result was worthwhile is incontrovertible too.

The book is divided into two sections: the first telling the story of Judith's development, and ending with her graduation from university. The second part explains to all those who may come into contact with deaf people, whether on a professional or on a social level, the type of problems which may arise, and how one may best assist the deaf person to integrate into the normal hearing world.

To understand deafness I have included a short description of the ear, and commented on what a hearing aid is, and how it works. There are chapters on lip-reading and the social difficulties which the deaf have to face. There are sections devoted to the education of a deaf child, which stress the importance of conversation, music, memory training and reading. Finally, integration of the less severely handicapped deaf child into mainstream education is considered, and the importance of providing adequate support for parents is stressed.

I have endeavoured throughout to provide relevant information in a simple straightforward manner, as it is my earnest wish that the problems of a largely neglected section of the community should be fully recognised and appreciated.

GLOSSARY

ATU An *auditory training unit*, whereby the sound of the human voice, speaking into a microphone, is considerably enhanced, and fed into the child's ear via headphones

audiometer A *pure tone audiometer* is used to compare a deaf person's ability to listen with that of a normal hearing person (standardised performance). The relationship is expressed in decibels. By varying the frequency of the pure tone administered, the ability at selective points throughout the spectrum of speech frequencies can be examined

conductive deafness Conductive deafness arises when the outer and/or middle ear is not functioning correctly. Sounds become quieter before they can reach the inner ear, but are not unduly distorted. While the various causes can often be overcome medically, a suitable hearing aid can effectively restore normal hearing should the medical measures fail

otosclerosis A degenerate condition which *initially* results in abnormal bone growth in the middle ear. This bone growth affects the movement of the ossicular chain and thereby induces a conductive hearing loss

perceptive deafness Perceptive deafness arises due to a malfunction at, or beyond, the middle ear. It may be caused by maldevelopment, damage or deterioration with age; while amplified sound may get the system to function, a degree of distortion is introduced which is related to the scale of abnormality that exists

Phonic Ear   A sophisticated hearing aid which has a remote microphone that can be worn by a chosen speaker. This remote microphone is linked to the hearing aid by radio, thereby ensuring that the speech of the chosen person is delivered with maximum clarity

profound deafness   A perceptive deafness so severe that, while suitable amplification can be provided, the distortion introduced by the abnormality still leads to serious auditory problems. In addition, should profound deafness occur before language has been developed, severe educational and social problems will arise

Part One

JUDITH

Chapter One

THE PERFECT SPECIMEN

March 1961

She lay flat on her back in the shiny black pram. Each time the small, chubby fist punched the pram beads strung across it, the pram rocked gently on its hinges. I stood in the dining-room window listening to the gurgles of glee that accompanied the frantic punching; I smiled happily to myself. This then was what it was like to have a *good* baby, not one that suffered in the early stages from seemingly endless problems with wind. Not one that was forever restless, never wanting to sit on one's knee and be cuddled. This, at last, was the perfect specimen; a baby who was content to lie and kick, endlessly curling and uncurling her fingers. Gurgling at the trees, the clouds, the baubles strung across her pram; chortling happily at whatever she saw.

May 23rd

I held her upright, her fat, soapy little body propped up against my arm in the bath. The plump legs kicked joyously towards the plastic yellow duck. The water slopped vigorously around. The bathroom door opened suddenly with a loud crack. Good! Daddy was home to see how she could nearly make it on her own. The plump little legs went on kicking. The plastic duck rocked violently. 'Hello, darling,' I said. Not turning. Not taking my eyes off the eager little face so preoccupied with its splashing. 'Look, she can nearly sit up.' My husband came round me to look at her from the front. Immediately the tiny face beamed up at him. The legs stopped their furious activity. She was all Daddy's.

Somewhere at the back of my mind a niggling suspicion began to grow, and would not be silenced. 'Could you do that again do you think?' I said. 'Do what?' my husband murmured. 'Go out and come in again.' 'Well all right, but why?' 'I'll tell you in a minute – just do it – please.' My husband turned away. I picked up the yellow duck and held it in front of Judith's face. The eyes focused, the chubby fist reached out, the voice chortled with delight. The door cracked open loudly. The eyes never left the plastic duck and, in that instant, I knew.

We went through the usual channels, of course. And we were lucky, very lucky. Within a week I had been to the clinic, for the routine weigh-in. It was tea-time while we were there and as luck would have it the nurse on duty dropped her teaspoon with a loud clatter. Judith, on the scales, made no response whatever. 'Well, that's not a nervy baby,' said the nurse. 'No,' I replied quietly. 'We think she is deaf.' Immediately the careless look was replaced with one of the utmost concern. 'Do you?' she said. 'Could you just sit over there a minute and wait.' Within seconds she was back, in her hand a cup, a teaspoon and some tissue paper. 'I'm just going to try a little test,' she said. 'You sit there, hold her on your knee and I'll go behind you.' I held Judith firmly and watched her eyes. The teaspoon clattered, the paper rustled but Judith's eyes never flickered, her head never turned. 'Well now,' said the nurse. 'She's probably OK, but I think we'd better have another opinion.'

Miss B came three days later. She was calm, authoritative and sympathetic. There were more tests and the same result. Miss B had been on a course at Manchester. She knew what she was talking about. She was not afraid to mention hearing aids. Hearing aids! On a baby of eight months! 'Oh yes,' she said. 'Especially on a baby of eight months. The early years are vital.' My stomach heaved. I had never seen a hearing aid. How would we manage?

The doctor came the next day. He looked at her eyes – no, I prayed, not her eyes too. But mercifully the eyes were all right. 'I think we must get an otologist to look at her,' he said. An otologist – what was that? Yes, of course, ears – it must be. Reeling thoughts raced through my mind. Yes, when? 'Soon,' I said. We must know soon.

June 7th

The specialist sat impersonally behind a large oak desk. He questioned severely, autocratically. Rubella? Jaundice? 'No,' I said, 'not rubella.' But was it? My mind flashed back 14 months. April 1960. Philip covered in spots. But the doctor had said no, hadn't he. And after all it was too late for that – the first three months wasn't it? Jaundice – yes – she was jaundiced at birth – I knew that because they wouldn't let me see her. A virus? Oh no, not just a virus. I didn't know that could do it. Yes, I remembered being ill in the January. I had gone to get a perm in town. And the girl had sneezed all over me, all the time. And then, for a fortnight after, I had been ill, really ill. We didn't get a doctor because we didn't know one; we had just moved house. And after all what was flu. I had no idea that I was pregnant. I had no idea that that could happen.

The specialist finished his questioning. He reached for the set of pipes on his desk. He went behind Judith and blew the pipes softly one after the other. He clapped loudly, several times. There was nothing; nothing.

Gravely the specialist returned and for the first time he addressed us both directly. 'I can't be certain,' he said. 'She is so young. But you must assume that she is profoundly deaf. That way, it can only get better, can't it, if you find there is something there after all.' 'An operation?' we murmured. 'Perhaps,' he said, 'if the damage lies in the middle ear – but not if the auditory nerve itself is damaged. You must assume she is deaf. You must start to train her now, tonight when you get home. The early years are very important. I will put you in touch with the pre-school deaf clinic and with the National Deaf Children's Society.'

I clutched Judith to me and we walked down the drive. At the gate the specialist called my husband back. 'What did he say?' I asked, as we drove home. 'He said you would need all the support you could get,' said my husband. And for the first time the tears came. 'It's silly,' I said, 'but I think I would like to do something we don't usually do. There are some strawberries in that shop. Let's have some. I know they're expensive but I feel like a treat.' We bought the strawberries and we went home. And the long uphill struggle commenced.

Judith at three months – not much animation here!

One year old: at Scarborough with Frances and Philip

Chapter Two

FINDING OUT

June 28th

The specialist moved quickly and we were given an appointment for St James's Hospital in Leeds. I held her squirming on my knee while the technician filled her ear with the uncomfortable wax. Her legs flailed violently as I tried hard to hold her still. It was important, wasn't it, to get a good impression. If she had to wear a hearing aid at least it should be one that would fit.

July 11th

Judith sat up for the first time on her own. Her second little white tooth was nearly through. She was beginning to grab hold of plastic plates and tins of powder. She was just like the others.

July 12th

We had our first visit to the pre-school deaf clinic. I pushed Judith in the pushchair down the steep hill to the station and we caught the diesel to Leeds. Then we found our way through the maze of streets to the dark brown painted door at the back of the Town Hall. I was nervous. This was the day I was going to learn how to put the hearing aid on. The specialist had advised us to wait until our first visit to the clinic. Mrs N was welcoming and reassuring. She talked to Judith and she talked to me. I learnt a lot that day. The importance of always sitting with the light on one's face, so that the child could lip-read properly. The importance of moving one's eyes to an object as one said the name, but never pointing.

The importance of repetition, and the importance of always making sure the child was watching before one spoke. I went home determined that whatever I could do for Judith that I would do. And the hearing aid became a part of our life.

July 26th

We combined a visit to a sick aunt with one to the National Deaf Children's Society. I had heard of Mrs Bloom and all she had done for her deaf daughter and I was anxious to meet her. Mrs Bloom's advice was definite: 'Remember that first and foremost this is a normal child. Treat and discipline her as such, always bearing her limitations in mind but never dwelling on them. Repetition, repetition and yet more repetition.' She was hopeful and she gave me hope.

August 1st

The first copies of *Talk* magazine arrived from the National Deaf Children's Society. I carried the playpen out into the garden and put Judith in it while I sat and read. There were articles about other deaf children. I devoured them avidly. What a lot they had achieved – would Judith be like that?

Frances and Philip were recovering from measles. They sat up in bed crayonning pictures. I went in and out of the house turning over the records of 'Pooh' and 'Cinderella' to keep them happy. Judith played contentedly with her toys. Every now and then I picked one up, held it to my face and said, 'Teddy. Here's Teddy. Nice Teddy. Mummy love Teddy. You have Teddy. There, put Teddy to bed.' She chortled happily.

August 4th

A relief doctor came to see Frances and Philip. He mentioned the possibility of getting an ear-mould for both ears. Perhaps that would be better? We didn't know.

August 14th

I wrote to Miss F asking what books, courses, etc. I could follow. She replied quickly, within two days. The courses were impossible; I couldn't leave the other children. But the books at least I could get. I wrote off to the Royal National Institute for the Deaf. I wrote to Mrs N. She gave me titles of books by the Ewings. I had complained about the ear-mould always dropping out. She said that the first one often did this but the later ones should be better. A little strip of plaster might help to hold it on. She said she would see me after the holidays. She reminded me to keep on chatting to Judith.

August 23rd

There was a programme on ITV – 'World of Silence'. There were deaf children talking on it but I couldn't understand what they said. Would Judith talk like that? I felt depressed.

August 26th

A big fat parcel of books arrived from the RNID. I tore off the brown wrappings eagerly. Four books: *Tim and His Hearing Aid*, *If Your Child is Deaf*, *Your Deaf Child* and *Through the Barriers of Deafness*. How would I ever find time to read them all? But I must. They were full of information about deafness. And I knew nothing, nothing at all.

August 29th

A dreadful day. Frances had a septic finger and wouldn't have it bathed, becoming hysterical at the very thought. Philip had one of his usual tantrums too. Even Judith was cross, cutting her fourth tooth.

The Superintendent of the Deaf called in the afternoon. He said Judith should go to a residential school because only that would give her the necessary discipline. He said it was too easy to spoil a child that was 'different'. He said that deaf children always ate noisily, dragged their feet, spoke monotonously. He said that the deaf should mix only with the deaf. No! No! I didn't believe it. I wouldn't believe it. That's not what they'd said in the NDCS in London. She *would* talk. She *would* mix. She *would* be normal. She was our child, not theirs, and we would *make* her normal.

August 30th

I took Judith to Leeds again for another mould. She was bigger now and I found it hard to hold her. She howled and howled and in the end we had to abandon the attempt. I came home on the train with her, feeling very dispirited.

September

The books helped. They helped enormously because they told me what to do. The other children were at school now and I had time to read. I made the time, because this was important. The housework could wait. Time to talk to Judith. Time to play. We had a box with 20 things – a ball, a swan, a horse, a shoe, a dog, a little lamb. I didn't know then that I could have chosen them better; that there were too many words of one syllable, too many words with an invisible 's', too many words that were indistinguishable for lip-reading. But perhaps it didn't really matter. She sat and she watched and she loved it all. We went through the same 'Teddy' routine with each one, and she gazed at my face with rapt attention. She couldn't yet crawl, which was a blessing; she just sat and watched on her large, fat bottom, her eyes never leaving my face, and gradually, very gradually, as my eyes flicked over to Teddy, or the horse propped up by the fireplace, so hers would follow suit, and I knew that somewhere within the unfathomable depth of her mind understanding was beginning.

Chapter Three

ONE YEAR OLD

Autumn 1961

Three times a day, for 15 minutes at a time, Judith and I went through the same routine. Out of the box came all the 20 articles one by one, the ball, the shoe, the doggy, the spoon, the beloved Teddy and all the others. 'Peep-bo Teddy. Oh, Teddy's gone! Where's Teddy? He's in the box again. Here he is. Hello Teddy. There. Mummy love Teddy. Frances love Teddy. Judith love Teddy. Teddy sit there. Bye-bye Teddy.' And so, little by little, as we finished talking to them, the row of toys grew in length. And one by one we put them all away, but not, of course, before we'd talked to them all over again. Having Frances or Philip there seemed, at first, a natural thing to do – but not for long! The distraction was too evident, Judith's interest in their own little faces too keen, and so, regretfully, I decided it had to be one to one. And then, of course, we faced another problem – how could I give her all this extra attention, and at the same time make absolutely sure that the others wouldn't feel resentment and jealousy? While they were at school it was easy enough, but there had to be a night-time session too, in order to split up the three short periods of learning, and that is when I blessed the other children's interest in 'Blue Peter' and 'Crackerjack'. They didn't need Mother around while following the doings of Petra or Leslie Crowther, and so Mother and Judith slid off into the kitchen to make their own kind of fun. Because it was the end of the day we spent less time on the static watching of the 'Teddy routine' and more on the nursery rhyme angle. I tried always to use rhymes with plenty of movement and, wherever possible, with words that were intelligible. 'Two

Little Dickie Birds' was a hit right from the start; so were 'Pat-a-Cake', 'This Little Piggy' and 'One, Two, Three, Four, Five –once I caught a fish alive', and we always finished up with 'This is the Way the Ladies Ride' with her fat little body enjoying the gradual quickening of pace and the gay abandonment of the final line.

She was babbling constantly now – 'dad-dad-dad', 'ba-ba-ba', and it seemed as if she heard herself through the hearing aid. That had become part of her standard equipment. It went on with her clothes in the morning and only came off when she went to bed. We had a further visit to the hospital to get an ear-mould, and this time Judith was more co-operative and an impression was taken of each ear.

While in Leeds we visited the School for the Deaf and were very taken with the beautiful surroundings and the excellent facilities enjoyed by the children. My dread of Judith having to attend a 'special school' at some time in the future was dispelled. Did it really matter *where* she went to school as long as she had every chance of learning?

Towards the end of September, Philip and Judith changed roles. For over four years we had never had a through night's sleep, as Philip seemed to be troubled by frequent nightmares and woke constantly. Now, at last, at four and a half, his wakefulness died away, but seemingly determined to fill the gap, Judith now woke and screamed in agony. This was an easier problem to deal with, however, because her own need was obviously for light. She could not hear our approaching footsteps or our soothing words and must have felt horribly isolated on the occasions when she woke during the night. We did not want to create bad habits by leaving the electric light on, but we found that an old-fashioned slow-burning night-light was worth its weight in gold at such times, and was to prove invaluable whenever she slept in strange surroundings in her early childhood.

At the end of September Judith was one year old, and I took her to the clinic for a check-up. On the whole we were pleased with her physical development. She couldn't stand or crawl but she swivelled around with quite a lot of dexterity, and the fact that she was content to sit made her a whole lot easier to talk to! One thing puzzled me, however. She was very, very slow at wanting to feed herself and she regarded things held out to her with a fair degree of suspicion, never attempting to grab them, but expressing interest simply by flapping her hands and kicking her feet. Had she become so dependent on me for cues that she was losing her own initiative, I wondered. (I needn't have worried!)

She was a noisy breather but that filled me only with a hope which I knew was probably misplaced. Maybe, I thought, it was adenoids that accounted for a good deal of the deafness. Maybe removing them would give her some degree of hearing. At all events we needed to know.

By October I could double the lesson sessions to 30 minutes at a time, three times a day, and by putting plenty of expression and appropriate actions into the nursery rhymes could retain her interest throughout. We started out by my just cuddling her and singing 'I Had a Little Nut-Tree', 'Baa, Baa, Black Sheep' and 'Twinkle, Twinkle Little Star' into her hearing aid. I am no opera singer, and in any case I know now that exact pitch and tone didn't really matter. What *did* matter and what somehow got through, were the rhythm and phrasing in my voice. That and the obvious interest I had in her; the birthright of any child. From just singing we went on to swaying, as we did 'See-Saw Margery Daw' and 'Rock-a-Bye Baby' and finally we put everything we'd got into 'Pat-a-Cake' and 'This is the Way'.

In October I took Judith for the third time to the pre-school deaf clinic. Judith was teething and not at all happy, neither during our journey – she screamed loudly each time the diesel hooted, and as there were four tunnels to negotiate the hootings were fairly frequent! – nor on our arrival at the clinic, where she had obviously decided this was to be a non-co-operating day; a day for sitting tearfully on the sidelines. However, there were compensations. At the clinic I heard for the first time of a new Amplivox Hearing Aid which would amplify the lower notes and might help Judith.

Mrs N promised to pursue the matter. And that evening Judith at last decided that she would sample bread and jam, but only if offered; picking it up from her own tray was still apparently a non-starter.

By the middle of November there was no doubt that Judith knew the lip-read pattern of 'ball'. I thought at the time that she had learnt this word first of all because of its obvious play associations. Now I know that it was the easiest to lip-read. She was 50 per cent certain on 'Teddy' and also on 'Bobby', 'horse', 'hat', 'shoe', 'pussy', 'doggy' and 'little lamb', nine out of our boxful of 20 articles – not too bad really I thought, after six months' work. Not bad at all I know now; only 'ball' and 'shoe' were easy, and 'Teddy' and 'doggy' virtually indistinguishable!

She seemed to brighten up immediately her hearing aid was switched on, but she no longer started to babble, and I noticed a worrying thing – if she were left alone at any time she immediately fell silent. There were times, of course, when she *had* to be left alone, but to counteract this I gave her a mirror. We had often looked in a mirror while she sat on my knee and I sang to her, and now the mirror on the floor seemed to produce the same effect. She started to babble again – not all the time, but whenever she caught sight of her own reflection.

She was crawling now, and it was more difficult to catch her attention, but at least the new mould fitted better and wasn't always falling out.

By December, Judith had decided that watching for lip-reading was just a waste of time, and getting up and down was far more interesting. She wouldn't watch for more than two minutes at a time, but by now she could recognise 10 words purely by lip-reading and I was sure that progress would return.

We had a visit at this time from Dr F, a psychologist from Leeds. He came at the suggestion of Mrs Bloom, and his visit was most helpful in that he reinforced what we had already noticed – namely that the psychological problems were not necessarily going to be with Judith, who was so far largely free of them, but could well occur in her brother and sister. It made us doubly determined that Frances and Philip should not suffer in this way, and in ensuring that, my husband was of the utmost help. He gave them the extra attention that I perforce had to devote to Judith, and in doing so we achieved the richest of all rewards – a united family and a united front.

Chapter Four

A DAY TO REMEMBER

1962

In January we paid several visits to Leeds in connection with obtaining a more powerful aid than the State Medresco, which was issued to every deaf child at that time. This Amplivox had first been mentioned as a possible help to Judith in October 1961. It was to be May 1962 before we finally obtained it. We were not particularly well off, the aid was expensive, and we decided to go through the usual channels of doctor, specialist and Local Authority. Had we known just how much difference it would make to Judith, and how very vital time was, we might well have agitated more, but even so we were lucky to obtain it by the time Judith was only one and a half. Our ignorance at this time was still quite extensive. We watched a surgical operation for otosclerosis on TV, performed using a microscope, and I wondered whether the realignment of the three small bones in the middle ear would be of any help to Judith. Parents always clutch at straws, and, though we had been told that the damage was probably in the inner ear and that this was inoperable, it was inevitable, I suppose, that we clung to the word 'probably' and hoped that some of the deafness at least was due to malfunctioning in the middle ear.

In the meantime the lessons went on and Judith continued to make progress, but in rather a see-saw kind of way, hampered as she was by frequent heavy colds. She was beginning, however, to show an interest in books, and we spent hours together looking at pictures and 'talking' about them. As a picture book of farm animals seemed to be her favourite, I bought her a miniature cow and horse to help to teach her the difference.

In March, at one and a half, she walked for the first time, and obviously thought it tremendously clever. She spent all morning practising, much to the delight of her brother and sister, who were overjoyed that she had considerately waited until a Saturday morning when they were at home to celebrate!

She seemed to be normal physically in most respects; the only thing that worried me was her continuing reluctance to feed herself. She would *not* pick the food up from her tray, and if it was put into her hand she would simply wave it around or throw it away again. She would take her mouth to the food but never the food to her mouth and she would make no attempt to clasp a cup – even when her hands were placed round it. If I left the food in front of her and walked away, she simply became hysterical and screamed blue murder, quite unlike her usual sunny-natured self. Again I wondered – had she become too dependent on myself? Since I had deliberately brought her up to watch my face all the time for the word of command, was she incapable of taking the initiative? I became so worried I asked for the paediatrician to come to see her, but when he came he was most reassuring and said it was purely developmental, and indeed within a week Judith was feeding herself with bread and butter, although she was almost two before she could use a spoon.

Perhaps she was far too busy at this time concentrating on another major breakthrough – her first word. Suddenly, on 9 April, when she was 19 months old, she looked out of the window and said quite decisively, 'ar'. I rushed excitedly to the window and indeed a blue car had just disappeared down the street. With fingers that shook I fumbled in the toy box and pulled out a little blue Dinky toy – 'Yes,' I said, 'it's a car. Look, *this* is a car. It's a blue car, and here's another.' I flicked over the pages of her picture book until we got to the right page. Very firmly her pudgy finger plonked itself on the illustration. 'Ar,' she said, distinctly and loudly. I hugged her closely to myself. The others were all out and there was no one to share my immediate joy, but this manifestation of the dawn of understanding was indeed a day to remember.

It was $10\frac{1}{2}$ months since we had first found her to be deaf. For all that time I had gone on pumping words in, and now at last, and not much later than a hearing child, she had given back her first word, her first attempt at two-way communication. Within two weeks we had 'a' for 'hat' and 'owers' for 'flowers', to be closely followed by 'uh-uh-uh-uh' implying 'bunny rabbit'.

Her lip-reading had come on enormously too. She knew 'bath' and 'boat' and 'fish' and 'swan', because bathtime was yet another wonderful opportunity for seizing her attention. She knew 'brush' and 'shoe' and 'hat' from the times we talked as we put on her clothes together. She knew 'monkey' and 'lamb' and 'frog' from the toy box, and she knew 'Dada' and 'Philip' – but not 'Frances', the 's' sounds were too difficult to lip-read.

Because she had been static for so long, and because, too, I was working largely by intuition, I had not taught her any 'doing words', as I could and should have done. Even while she was sitting, we could have had 'clap' and 'throw', 'roll' and 'fetch', 'open' and 'close' and many, many more. One verb only she knew – love – but perhaps it was significant of the world that surrounded her that this was the first 'doing' word she was conscious of, for there *was* love, a great deal of it, not only from those who were closest to her but from the extended family as well.

During all her early years, which could have been a time of great stress for me, the extended family – and in particular her grandparents and a very close aunt – were of tremendous physical help, minding the other children, so that I could take Judith to Leeds to the clinic, meeting us back on the train, so that I no longer had the long pram-push up a very steep hill; sitting in, so that I could have the occasional trip to the shops on my own, and sometimes looking after Judith so that the remaining four of us could enjoy a walk together. Psychologically this helped a very great deal. The task of teaching Judith, of going over and over the same repetitive words, never became irksome or dull, because I was reasonably fresh when I tackled it. We suffered, as most families with young children do, from seemingly endless broken nights, from perpetual coughs, colds and earaches, from frayed tempers and squabbles and sulks, but they never seemed insurmountable or insupportable because I was always sustained by those around me. I knew there would be another day and a renewed opportunity.

Chapter Five

HELP FROM ABROAD

At Christmas we had corresponded, as we usually did, with our Australian cousins, and in the course of the letter had spoken of Judith's deafness and of how we were tackling it. In the spring, back came a letter giving me yet further hope, for cousin Elizabeth had found out some information about a clinic in America that ran a correspondence course. She gave me the address, and in May I wrote to the John Tracy Clinic in Los Angeles to ask if we could enrol on their course.

In the meantime, while we waited for their reply, we decided to take a holiday. This was the first holiday we had had since we had discovered that Judith was deaf, and we wondered how she would react away from her familiar surroundings. To avoid a long and tiring journey we decided to fly to the Isle of Man, and within two hours we were within the hotel. So far, so good, but it was to prove the most restless holiday my husband and I ever had! Fortunately the weather was fine, and Frances and Philip quite content to play on the beach, but not Judith, Oh no! I have learnt since that deaf children do tend to be intensely curious and physically very active, and nothing would content Madam but that we should spend the entire holiday on the move. First my husband, holding Judith firmly by the hand, would set off along the beach, up the steps, along the promenade, down the steps, and back to the starting point. Whereupon a handover would take place and it would be my turn, while he helped Frances and Philip to make sand castles.

I don't think we sat down together throughout the entire holiday, for when I thought her chubby little legs must surely be tired from so much walking, her adventurous spirit was anything but ready to sit still, and off we would go again – in the pushchair this time. We had deliberately acquired one that faced the pusher, as this way it was possible to talk to her as we went along and to draw her attention to all the things we saw. We did see a lot that holiday. The other children needed to be occupied in the afternoon if they were to amuse themselves in the morning, and so we went to Castletown on the bus, to Rushton Abbey on the train, and one day we hired a car and saw the Laxey Wheel, the lighthouse at Aire and the majestic beauty of Snaefell. All of them experiences for Judith, to be stored away in her memory, to be recalled by postcards and photographs, and to provide endless talking points for the future.

Our only real difficulty was that Judith, in strange surroundings, was very much more afraid of the dark, but we solved this by always leaving a night-light burning. By the end of the week she had regained her confidence and we were able to take the other children out on the last night for a final treat. I was nervous about leaving her, even though I knew the hotel would baby-sit, but we were determined that the others should never suffer from her handicap, and that she should never be treated differently just because she was deaf.

Like any normal child she had her ups and downs. She did not like her hair cut, she was miserable in cafés, and she was sometimes quite unpredictably cross and would screech and screech. Whenever we could, we tried to find out the reason, and put things right, but no parents are paragons, and when we thought we had done all we could, and it was just sheer naughtiness, then she would get a tap or a telling off just as firmly as the other two.

I was helping at this time to run a church play centre for pre-school children. As Judith was now one and three-quarters, I thought it would help her to mix as much as possible with other children and took her with me. Most of the time she fitted in very well. If she didn't, then we left early, but gradually she learnt to adapt to the other children, and when, later in the summer, we started a Tufty Club, she learned to watch the others closely, to do exactly what they did, and to wait her turn to cross on the zebra crossing.

In July I received the first two lessons from the John Tracy correspondence course and found that Judith was well up to scratch. Her lip-reading was progressing, and I could talk to her now in quite long sentences – 'Shall we go and find your bath?' 'Sit down and let Mummy put your shoe on', and she would show by her actions that she understood what I was talking about. Speech-wise she had not made much progress, but with all that physical activity this was not really surprising. She had added a 'sh-sh' sound, meaning shoes, but otherwise there was nothing new. She did, however, make some sort of grunty noise for everything we talked about, and this was all to the good, for it meant she realised the importance of speech, even if she couldn't achieve it. As suggested by the Tracy Clinic, I started making a large coloured scrapbook for Judith at this time, with all kinds of pictures in, and she learnt very quickly to match up the objects round the house to the pictures in the book. A sister-in-law, who was artistic, made us a very special picture book, and this was a real joy because it was undoubtedly *her* swing in the garden in all the right colours, *her* red stool and even *her* flight of steps with the rail at the side! The John Tracy Clinic suggested colour-matching games that I had not yet tried – dropping red, yellow and blue balls into red, yellow and blue beakers. Judith showed interest and sometimes got them right and sometimes not, but I suspected that she was far more interested (quite rightly!) in enjoying dropping the balls into the beakers than in trying to match the colours, so we left it for the time being and I tried her out later with less toy-like materials.

I also bought her a brightly coloured picture lotto and presented her with one card and five smaller pictures which appeared on the card, making sure to choose things with which she was familiar – a chair, a table, a clock and so on. The first day she got very upset, because although she seemed to know where she wanted to put them she couldn't cover the pictures neatly. Not surprising, as she was not yet two, and manipulating her fingers was not her strong point. I put them away, and the next day I cut up the big card, spread the same five pictures round the room and let her throw the matching picture on top. Ah! This was much more fun! – and by September we could tackle 10.

In September, too, we had another short holiday, staying with friends in Scotland. This time Judith was much less restless and enjoyed dropping little stones into the loch; even though she couldn't hear the 'plop', the circular ripples seemed to amuse her. We encountered another problem on the way home. Judith had a hearty appetite, there was nothing the matter with her sense of smell, and in a roadside café, when she could both see and smell food, she could not understand why it was not immediately available on her plate. The concept of 'soon' was a difficult one to understand at that stage, and my husband and I spent a difficult half-hour taking turns in walking up and down with her on the road outside, glancing ever-hopefully through the window every five minutes to see if the food had arrived!

If it did nothing else, that experience convinced us that patience was a lesson she was just going to have to learn – not easy for a two-year-old. She was very, very determined and she was devoted to routine. Everything had to be done in exactly the same order. Because, in the beginning, we had propped up her toys in a row as we talked to them, so now we had to have all her toys grouped round her before we could start looking at a book. Because she presumably equated going on a train with going inside a house, we had to take off coat, hat, scarf, gloves and trousers before we could begin to enjoy the journey – and of course they all had to be put on again 20 minutes later in time to get off the train at Leeds. She could not bear open doors, toys that fell over, or anything untidy, but on the plus side she would play by herself for an hour or more, she was not too 'mummified' and would accept Daddy's company instead, and she adored Frances and Philip. All in all we were well pleased with the progress our little two-year-old had made.

Chapter Six

ONE OF THE FAMILY

For the next six months Judith continued to make steady progress. The inquisitive side of her nature came well to the fore, and she was no longer content to play quietly by herself. She much preferred to trot around the house, and rapidly became an expert, if left alone, at emptying cupboards and drawers, removing books, even dancing on tables and the window-sill! She was extremely determined and would climb into her own high chair for meal times; no shut door was an obstacle, for she quickly discovered she had only to drag a chair near enough to open it, and if she 'needed' a certain heavy toy upstairs she would drag it there herself rather than asking for help. All this fantastic energy needed to be harnessed. Cheerful, strong-willed and mischievous, she trotted round the house after me, sweeping, dusting, polishing. She brought her little chair to stand at the sink with me and 'help' to wash up, or clean the vegetables. And all the time we talked about what we were doing. 'Put the spoons in the water. That's right. Now we'll put some soap in. Mix it up. Look, lots of bubbles. Aren't they funny? Here's a cloth. You help Mummy. Pull the spoon out. That's right. Now rub it on the cloth. Look, like this, to make it dry.' etc. etc. etc. All day long. And if the jobs took three times as long, which they usually did, well it didn't really matter, for she was learning all the time.

We still went on with our 'lesson times' as well of course. By December she could match over 40 objects to cards. We also tried a sense-training exercise with objects hidden in a bag which the Tracy Clinic had recommended. For some reason Judith didn't like this; she much preferred to *see* what we were talking about, and perhaps, remembering her slowness in feeding herself, her fingers were not particularly sensitive. She adored the rhythmic exercises I tried with her, holding her in my arms and swaying to music, but she wouldn't hold hands and dance. As the clinic suggested, I tried her out with listening to all kinds of sounds – drums, gongs, whistles – but there was not much response at this stage, and she greatly preferred snuggling up close and being sung to.

Lip-reading practice went on all day long, as she 'helped' me around the house but we also made time to do definite exercises. The lotto cards were useful here too. I would take one in my hand and say the word, without showing her the picture, and she would take great delight in running for the boat or the basket, the shoes or the spoon. She mixed up some things, of course, 'glasses' could just as well be 'carrots' and I accepted them as such; the important thing was that she was *enjoying* the experience.

When I was exhausted I sat down with a book and she would bring her little chair – a second birthday present, and a useful one – and sit near me. We would turn over the pages together and talk about what we saw, and before very long she would be off again. A spoon demanded a run into the kitchen, the dragging of a stool to the drawer, the triumphant opening of the drawer and the waving of the spoon in the air to the cry of 'oon', whereas for an egg, fortunately, she contented herself with waving at the pantry!

She was now completely at home at the Thursday play centre, sharing and co-operating all the time and obviously greatly enjoying the company of the other children. I made holes in all her little dresses, so that she could wear the hearing aid in its harness, *underneath* her dress, but with the microphone still exposed through the hole. That way the other children were less conscious of it, and also it no longer nose-dived out of its pocket when she leant forward.

She loved the times when Frances and Philip were home from school. If she couldn't play the same games with them, at least she could play in the same room, and they were very good with her, accepting her company patiently and entering into her play. As soon as I had got through the tasks that had to be done we went out together up the Bank, or even, if there was time, up to the moors. On Saturday afternoons, when Daddy was home, we went shopping in Harrogate to see the fairy lights, we visited Father Christmas in Bradford, we went sliding during a cold snap on

Ilkley Tarn, and we saw the bridge at Bolton Abbey hanging with icicles, with huge ice floes gleaming on the river.

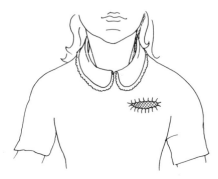

A little hole was cut in all Judith's dresses

On Sundays we tried always to go to church together. If there was a Parade Service and something to watch, then Judith stuck it out, if not, then Daddy or I would remove her when she became restless, but quite often, with the help of a book to look at, she managed to see it through, and after the service my husband would frequently take all three of the children for a walk through the woods.

During all this time Judith had a lot of contact with people, with the family particularly of course – grandparents, uncles, aunts were always visiting – but also with the children at the Tufty Club and strangers at church and in the shops. They knew she was deaf and were very good at smiling at her and saying something. Even though she obviously didn't understand what they said, she must have absorbed the idea that the world as a whole was a friendly place, and indeed it was to hold few terrors for her in the years to come. She accepted wholeheartedly the friendliness that people offered, and when, this particular Christmas, we invited Tom, an African student from the Cameroons, to share it with us, she revelled in the curliness of his hair and the wideness of his smile, storing away somewhere in her subconscious the fact that the colour of one's skin is hardly an important consideration.

It was obvious that she now had enough self-confidence to be ready for school, and although I viewed with some alarm the prospect of sending a two-and-a-half year old away for the whole day, I accepted that the constant presence of other children would be beneficial, and we arranged an appointment to see the school in Bradford.

Chapter Seven

OFF TO SCHOOL

We had already been, when Judith was only 10 months old, to visit the school at Leeds, but in January 1963 we decided to look at the Bradford School for the Deaf. We lived between the two areas, and could, at that time, have chosen either. At Leeds, the buildings had been purpose-built, the surroundings were beautiful, and the immediate impression had been a good one. Here, at Bradford, as it was then, our first sighting was very different. A big and rather gloomy old house, a severe stone staircase, long dark corridors, and a Head who seemed, on first acquaintance, to match the austerity of the building by the coldness of her personality. Gradually, however, as the afternoon wore on, and she devoted hour after hour to talking about deafness, to showing us the classrooms, to introducing us to the children, I began to realise that here was someone who really understood what deafness meant. As we went round the building, I became aware of the involvement of the staff and the eagerness of the children to talk to us. Miss V was showing a rabbit. The eager little faces of the six-year-olds were clamouring for attention, dying to tell her what they had noticed about its quivering face, its waving whiskers. It was the same upstairs in the cookery room. Hands shot up in the air as Miss B asked them what they were making. I couldn't always understand what they said, but their longing to communicate was so evident, their desire to be part of the normal world was so clear, there was no doubt at all in my mind that this was the school for Judith.

Miss B explained to us that the children came from a very wide area, not only from Bradford, but from Batley and Pudsey, Wakefield and Keighley, Huddersfield and Halifax. We began to have some idea of the size of the problem. She explained that

Judith would be picked up by taxi at 8.10 a.m. and that she must be ready when the taxi tooted, as there were five other children to collect from surrounding areas. She would be brought back again at about 4.15 p.m. Eight hours at school for a two-year-old! And eight hours without her company. I thought about how tired she would get, and how much I should miss her, and I wondered, not for the first time, if we were doing the right thing.

On 24 April, when she was two years and seven months, Judith started school. On the first day, I went with her in the taxi but I need not have worried. When we arrived in the nursery, Perry, a little auburn-haired boy, took her straight in tow, and together the two of them made off towards the rocking horse. My fears for Judith were groundless; the ache was only in my own heart.

For the rest of that year our life settled into its new pattern. Judith seemed quite happy to set off in the taxi each morning, but she was equally content at the weekend to be told, 'There is no school today', and she settled back into the old routine of sweeping and dusting, washing up and baking. When she came home at four o'clock she needed my exclusive attention for the first half-hour until she had had her tea, but then she would settle down again and enjoy playing with her toys. Once she had had an hour's play by herself she was quite ready to be withdrawn into the kitchen and delighted to go through our old nursery rhymes and singing games.

I waited eagerly for each instalment of the John Tracy correspondence course and devoured all that they said about encouraging speech. Every evening she sat on my knee and we looked in the mirror together while we talked about the farm animals. She loved this, and would try to imitate the noises the animals made: the 'woof-woof' for the dog, the 'moo' for the cow and the 'baa-aa' for the sheep. We made a book with pictures in it of things she knew that all began with 'b': a ball, a baby, a basket. She managed the 'b' sound very well but we never said it by itself; always within a word and that word usually within a sentence. 'Look here's a ball. Can you say *ball*?' In the same way we looked in the mirror together while I formed my lips into the right positions for 'oo' and 'ee' and she felt with her fingers the different shapes I made, and tried very hard to imitate them. She wasn't equally good on all the exercises, of course. She was particularly poor on 'mmm' and she couldn't blow feathers or ping-pong balls. I wondered yet again whether she wasn't unnecessarily handicapped by adenoids, and we asked for a further visit to the specialist. We had had a routine one the preceding January and I had been furious at wasting an entire afternoon while waiting one and a half hours for a five-minute interview, by which time Judith had been tired, cross and quite un-co-operative.

This time we did better, and were able to arrange for her adenoids to be removed. She went into hospital for this when she was three years and four months old. I had wondered how she would survive such a traumatic experience, but the nursing staff were most kind and understanding. I was allowed to stay with her for two hours until her 'op' was due and then was able to return just as she was coming round. As a result she came home just as happily as she went in, and if the removal of her adenoids made no difference to her hearing, it certainly helped her general health. She got far fewer colds and was much brighter in consequence, but the blowing remained a real problem and she was to be four and a half before she could manage it.

By the time she was three and a quarter I had completed all 12 instalments of the correspondence course, but the exercises, which were invaluable, I went on using for years, and have never ceased to be grateful for them. There is no doubt at all in my mind that they were the major stimulus in enabling me to help Judith in those very early days, the time when the acquisition of speech and language is all important. Her development mirrored closely the development of a normal child, but it was the correspondence course which provided the spur; it supplied a core of information, it pointed out pitfalls to avoid, and above all, through its very personal approach, it provided the encouragement which was so essential.

Chapter Eight

FOUR TO SIX

By the time Judith was three and a half I had become so interested in the development of deaf children that I decided to go in to the Bradford school one day a week. I wanted to learn as much as I could about the actual teaching of speech, and I felt that having helped Judith I could be of some use myself.

There were two immediate results from this. To teach in the same building as one's own child is not easy, but I tried always to keep out of Judith's sight as much as possible. It was nevertheless quite obvious that she was wrongly placed in the Nursery and I did interfere in this respect. In terms of age, of course, the Nursery was the right place for her, but she had gone into it with a quite extensive lip-reading vocabulary and with the desire and the ability to imitate speech to some extent. The other children, however, for various reasons, had very little communication, and I knew that Judith would make no further progress in speech unless she could be placed with older children. A month after I entered school she was transferred to Miss V's class and there was an immediate surge in her progress. She began to show a tremendous interest in both figures and letters. She learnt to count to 10 and she could pick out the individual figures, from the box, and arrange them in the right order, making appropriate noises as she put each one down on the table. In the same way she learnt to pick out letters from a box in order to match the print on newspaper headlines; she was very quick indeed at distinguishing shapes – P from R: C from G.

A further result of my entering school was that I was allowed to borrow an auditory training unit (ATU) (see p. 13), and to use it with Judith. This piece of equipment I soon found to be invaluable. Judith had no objection at all to wearing the

Say 'oo'! The daily practice on the ATU (photo reproduced with the permission of the *Telegraph & Argus*, Bradford)

headphones, and when I spoke to her through the microphone, because my voice was so much clearer to her, she responded instantly and would repeat 'Hello Mummy', 'Hello Frances', 'Hello Philip', quite distinctly. I realised that this was the most valuable tool we had yet found, and we decided to use a small legacy to purchase an Amplivox ATU of our own, so that we could have constant use of it. The price, £70, seemed a lot of money, but in what it did for Judith the machine proved to be worth a hundred times that amount. We used it constantly for the next seven years. All our lessons together took place using the headphones, and within a year she was imitating whatever I said much more clearly. She learnt to count to 50, she began to read, and she repeated short sentences. Unlike a hearing child of four and a half, she did not at this stage have *conversation*; that was to come later, when she was five. She simply repeated 'I am better', 'Philip is at school', 'I have a blue dress', and so on, but it was a beginning.

She was, through lip-reading, showing a great deal more understanding, and at this stage we were able to use some particularly significant words. For example: 'borrow' – 'Yes, it's Frances's, but you may borrow it.' or 'How many?' when laying the table for tea. 'Poorly' and 'better', 'lovely' and 'awful', 'heavy' and 'light', 'please' and 'thank you' were all words which came in every day. She was very dependent on her hearing aid, which she wore constantly. If it were broken, as inevitably happened on a number of occasions, and she had to go back to wearing the old Medresco, she became much quieter, and no longer chattered to herself as she played.

During all this fourth year of her life she continued to fit in with the other children both at school and at home. She had by now become thoroughly domesticated; she was an excellent and thorough washer-upper, and the fact that she undoubtedly played her part in the household chores made her all the more acceptable as far as Frances and Philip were concerned. They were very proud of their little sister and helped her in innumerable ways. They showed her how to build houses out of Lego, they played Pelmanism with her, they played with her in the garden, and they took care to look at her when they spoke, so that she could lip-read what they said. In the summer I found it possible to take all three of them out on day trips together, and we went to the swimming pool at Ilkley, to Filey one day and to Bridlington another. Because the other children sat and looked at books or crayonned pictures on the train, so did she, because she wanted above all to be like them. They were her idols; she copied what they did, and she was both accepting and accepted.

She was not at this time aware of her deafness at all. Her hearing aid went on as naturally as her clothes, and she never seemed unduly conscious of it (except when it was broken) or to have any concept of being 'different' in any way. We tried to extend her experience in as many directions as possible. She went with the others to 'help' them to choose new shoes or a new carpet for their bedroom. If there was a play or a show that was full of life and movement then we took her to it. When she was four and a half she went with the others to the shows we thought were suitable for them. The others were of an age to enjoy *Treasure Island*, and so Judith went too, not following much of the story, but undoubtedly enjoying the colour and the action. In the same way we took her to see *Snow White* but in this case it was easier, because we could look at the story in the book, both before and afterwards, and she was able to follow it much better. The cinema was a different matter. She went with the others to *The Sound of Music* but it was far more difficult to explain what was going on in a darkened cinema when she could not lip-read, and there were no intervals to break up the performance and to provide time for explanations.

In the same way the TV was not a great deal of use. Cartoons such as 'Tom and Jerry' she revelled in. There was plenty to see, the action was fast and furious, and she could follow what was going on. She enjoyed, too, the homeliness of 'Blue Peter', the familiar figures of Lesley or Peter, the pets, and the wonderful creations made from cornflake boxes or detergent bottles. She could *see* what their hands were doing, and the voices didn't really matter, but with other programmes the voices were all important, and without them the programmes were a meaningless jumble. She turned back to her books and her toys, and above all to the people around her; to a world she recognised, that was full of meaning.

She was five now and burning with curiosity. And at last she was talking spontaneously. When I said 'Goodnight Judith', she would change it round and reply 'Goodnight Mummy'; up to that point her speech had been mere repetition. She was full of life and very vivacious, and she wanted to know who?, what? and where? all the time. If some member of the family were missing, then she would immediately ask, 'Where's so-and-so?' When I was buying anything in a shop she would say at once, 'Who?', meaning 'Who is that for?' All this, I realised later, must have been an echo of the phrases she heard constantly at school: 'Who?', 'Where?', 'What?' 'What is . . . doing?' She was perfectly content as long as we supplied her with an answer, but she insisted on having one. On the rare occasions when she couldn't make herself understood she would get very upset and try to mould and push my face into the shape she was trying to represent.

When she was five and a quarter we decided to send her to Sunday School. This was the first time she had been on her own with hearing children, for at the Tufty Club I had always been there to refer to if necessary. For the first few weeks she was happy enough, and even won a prize as the 'Queen of Hearts' in the fancy dress competition. But although this gave her a temporary confidence, and she could equal the others in any colouring that had to be done, she could not understand the stories told or what the other children said: she was obviously unhappy, and regretfully we withdrew her, deciding that she was not yet ready for such an experiment.

She was very happy, however, at school, in an environment with which she was familiar, but at home she had a temporary phase of being much naughtier. She would not look up and listen for long, and although words were by now tumbling out, they were very indistinct, and her attempts at imitation were much poorer. When she was five and a half her annual check-up was due. An auditory test suggested that her left ear was slightly better than her right, but her left ear-mould had been broken for some weeks. Perhaps this accounted for her restlessness and lack of response? And indeed so it proved, for with the issue of new moulds – for which we had the inevitable long wait – Judith's attention span again improved, and she was willing to sit once more and work with the ATU.

Sunday walks are fun! Baildon, 1964

We looked at books together, we added more nursery rhymes and jingles to our list, and she tried very hard to say them too. She still had a lot of difficulty with breath control. She said a hard 'ch' instead of 'sh' and she couldn't manage 's' but there were some consonants now, 'b' and 'm', 'd' and 'n', 'l' and even 'p' and 'th' when she remembered how to get them. 'T' was very poor and so was 'k', but there was no doubt at all that she had improved enormously over the year.

When she was six and a quarter we saw the specialist, and he tested her again. He was pleased with her progress, but since she still did not respond to any but the lowest of notes on the audiometer, he confirmed his diagnosis that she was profoundly deaf. He said that the pleasing quality of her voice was due solely to the constant training she had received, and that there was no sign that her deafness was other than perceptive.

'I can talk too.' On a visit to her cousins

I suppose that up to that point I had always harboured some secret wish that she might prove to have a degree of conductive deafness; that damage to the middle ear was part of the cause, and that an operation might be possible in the future. Now, finally, it was evident that it was not to be so. No operation would ever help, the nerve cells of the inner ear were irretrievably damaged and she could only use what she had. But what a lot that was! How far she had come in the past five years! We looked forward to the future in a spirit of adventure and of hope.

Chapter Nine

CAN JULIA HEAR?

Our experience with Sunday School having failed, we resolved to look round for other ways of integrating Judith with hearing children. She still enjoyed the company of Frances and Philip, but as they grew older so they quite naturally acquired more and more of their own friends and were away from home more often. Besides, they were older than she was, and she needed the company of other six-year-olds.

We decided to try out a dancing class, for Judith adored movement and it would help her too, we thought, in acquiring a sense of rhythm. One Saturday, therefore, when she was six and a half we set off for Bradford. She was none too happy at first, but by the second week she had settled in and was attempting everything. As long as she could *see* what the teacher did she managed very well, but she was lost as soon as she had to turn her back and revolve on the spot. However she enjoyed the experience, and was to continue there for the next two years. It undoubtedly helped her to acquire a sense of rhythm and it added yet another dimension to the things she could do, and thus helped to build up her confidence. She would frequently dance round the room at home, and loved being asked to demonstrate her steps. She was not primarily an extrovert, indeed if anything she was somewhat shy, but she would respond to the attention anyone gave her as a flower opening to the sun.

By the time she was seven she was really enjoying stories. The Ladybird books were a boon here. She would put the headphones on and we would sit side by side. I would read a short phrase, pointing with my finger, and then she would say it after me while I pointed it out. We never read a whole sentence at a time unless it was a very short one because she could not have carried it in her auditory memory, but she could manage: One day a handsome prince – rode up to the dwarfs' house – When he saw Snow White – he fell in love with her at once, etc. She seldom told me if she didn't know what words meant; she seemed far more anxious to absorb the sense of what was happening, but time and again when I knew she couldn't possibly know the meaning of a word I would stop and explain it.

She chattered a lot now, but her speech was very indistinct. When she had the headphones on she imitated the 'k' and the 'n' sounds much better, but without them even the vowel sounds deteriorated: 'aw' to 'ar' and 'oo' to 'u'. She became at this stage very conscious of her deafness. She would often ask, 'Can you hear that?' and say, 'I not hear'; and one day I got a surprising insight into what she must have been thinking. She had always played with, and known, children older than herself – first her brother and sister, then the children at the Tufty Club. The children at dancing class were a little older, as were the two little girls next door, with whom she sometimes played. One day that summer we went to visit my brother's family at Skipton. We were walking through the fields with little cousin Julia, then fourteen months, in her pushchair. My sister-in-law spoke to Julia about the horses as we walked along. She spoke to her from the back, because the pushchair faced the other way, and Julia quite naturally turned round. In utter amazement Judith, who was by my side, said immediately, 'Can Julia hear?' And then, 'Can Julia see?' A lump came into my throat. She must have been thinking that hearing came as one grew older; that she had only to wait a year or so and she would be able to hear like everybody else.

Surprisingly enough, although I felt sad for her, the knowledge that she couldn't and wouldn't hear seemed to mean very little to Judith at this stage. She was content with what she *could* do. If there was nobody available then she would get a book and read to herself or do crayonning or jigsaws, but she loved company. She played French cricket with Frances and Philip and she adored playing with the twins next door, endless games of 'house' or dressing up, or more boisterously on bikes or with a ball.

She had made great strides at school. The classes in a school for the deaf are small – at the most 10 children – sometimes as few as six. The children sit in a horseshoe formation so that they can lip-read, and communicate, not only with their teacher, but also with each other. They wear headphones all the time they are conversing, so that they can receive the maximum amount of amplification of sound, and each child has its own microphone to speak to the others. Headphones can be tiring and restricting for young children, restlessness may create feedback – an irritating high-pitched whistle – but nevertheless maximum sound input is essential and makes an enormous difference to what the children are able to hear.

Judith was now in a class with 10 other profoundly deaf children, all but one older than she was, and she was being taught formally and consistently by Mrs H. From 'What colour is the button?' and 'What is Peter doing?', from 'Did the sugar cost more than the treacle?' and 'Does a teacher sell meat?' she had progressed to 'What kind of a car has your Daddy?' and 'What did Miss N say to Mrs H?' Question and answer formed a great part of the teaching, and all was recorded in written form, so that it could be referred to later. And she was asking quite reasoned questions now. On the moors she picked up a stone and said, 'Mummy – how grow?' and she demanded, when she saw a baby, 'Where from – how grow?'

That summer, although very young, she went with a school party to Kettlewell and came back brimming with vitality and conversation. She had obviously vastly enjoyed the experience, but then she took an intense delight in everything she did. We had a caravan now, and in August enjoyed a fortnight's holiday in Wales. She loved it all, sleeping in the caravan or in the little tent, helping to fetch the water, to peel the potatoes, to do the shopping. Bathing in the breakers, paddling in the pools, even walking through the Welsh drizzle, all were equally joyous to her; she never grizzled, she enjoyed to the full each experience as it came.

By this time I had embarked on training for the Diploma of Teachers of the Deaf. I was still only part-time, but for the past two years I had been going into school three days a week instead of only one. I used the remaining two days to study, and indeed I found the going very hard. I knew nothing of anatomy or audiology. The teaching of language and speech had all to be learned, and in addition I had not even been a teacher before Judith was born, so that even the theory of education was foreign to me.

I bought myself a tape recorder and found it of great value in recording Judith's speech and in attempting to analyse it. Poor girl, she was corrected much more frequently now that I knew what I was talking about! 'No, Judith, it's "Please may I have some more mil*k*",' I would say, or 'It's Yes-s-s; *you* are saying "Yech".' She needed these constant speech lessons however, for she was no longer reading out loud to herself or talking to her dolls as she played with them, like she used to do. All this talking to herself had been excellent; it had helped to keep the tone of her voice very natural, and she did it from being quite small. In the car, at two years old, she would 'count' the lamp-posts by saying 'ah-da' every time we passed one; an irritating habit but good for her voice. And at six years old, even while dressing herself, she would say 'What are now my clothes?' Now she became much more silent. Was it just the natural development of childhood, that the stage for talking to herself had passed, or was it that she was becoming more and more conscious of her deafness? At dancing class, where it was not so easy to hide the hearing aid in its harness under her clothes, she would edge away from inquisitive children who not unnaturally wanted to know what this strange thing was. She never attempted to make contact with them, and all too obviously she felt herself to be the 'odd one out'. Yet she loved the movement and the rhythm, and I was sure it was helping her speech. We resolved to try out another experiment.

We had a piano in the house, and although I was no musician I had used it for teaching Judith to listen, by playing first high notes and then low notes to see if she could discriminate at all. Now I wondered whether she could be taught to play herself. I approached a young local teacher who was extremely diffident at first. 'But how can I talk to her? How will she understand what I say?' she queried. 'Don't worry,' I replied. 'I'll be there, just outside, if you want me. *Show* her what you want her to do. She'll soon get the hang of it.' And indeed she did. And loved it. She learnt which finger to use for which note. Since she couldn't hear the sound if a finger went wrong, then she was wrong for the whole of the phrase, until she realised she'd got herself tangled up and sorted her fingering out, but it didn't matter. She had another thing she could take pleasure in. The rhythm and phrasing helped her speech, and since the little tunes had words to them she 'sang' the words (very much out of key but never mind) as she played, and thus started using her voice again. For several years this piano playing continued to give her a great deal of pleasure, and only became a burden when lessons crowded it out.

She practised both before and after breakfast and frequently at the weekend. She said she could 'hear', although it was difficult to determine what, but she always put on her headphones herself before she played. The set now lived on the top of the piano and she propped the microphone at the end of the keyboard. Rhythm really entered into her life and she went up the stairs thumping out 'Polly Put the Kettle on' or 'Jack and Jill'. Another dimension, and another step forward, for a seven-year-old who was determined to enjoy life.

Chapter Ten

GROWTH IN SPEECH AND LANGUAGE

The formal language teaching that Judith was receiving at school was now quite recognisable in the type of sentences she was using at home. 'What are my clothes?' had become, 'Mummy, what shall I put on?', a direct result of using the future tense in work-card after work-card at school. She used 'because' and 'if' and 'or' and 'shall I?' all the time. For instance she would say, 'I think I had better take my umbrella or I will get wet', and, 'Why don't you move your chair because there is no room for the trolley.' I would frequently come across her talking to herself at this time; perhaps in a muddle with her clothes, she would be saying, 'Where am I? What shall I do?', or if she were playing the piano and discovered at the end of the bar she had got it all wrong she would say to herself, 'Again, do it again.' I realised then that language had become a real part of her life; she used it all the time and it was fascinating to hear her talking in her sleep, even though, as with anybody else, *what* she said was indecipherable!

We decided that she must be encouraged to go shopping, and practise this new desire to speak. What she was saying, however, although quite clear to me, was going to be very difficult for the outside world to understand. Although the vowel sounds were reasonably clear, the consonants were blurred, faulty or sometimes missing altogether. 'T' had temporarily regressed to 'k' and 's' and 'sh' were quite definitely poor. I decided that the only thing to do was to prime the local shopkeepers, explain the difficulties, and ask them to encourage her as much as possible. She was, as I have said, not basically an extrovert, and I knew that any setback – thinking that someone was laughing at her, or feeling stupid because they couldn't understand her – would upset her terribly, and that would put the clock back years. And so I sent her out with a purse, a shopping basket and a written message to use if all else failed. The first time or two I rang the shopkeeper in advance to say what the request was going to be – cheating really, but I felt sorry for them as well as for her; it is not easy to attune to deaf speech if you have not heard it before.

I knew, when I saw her beaming face as she came back through the gate, that I had done the right thing. Nothing succeeds like success, and having managed the baker, she was ready now for the grocer. Within a week or two she was managing on her own and could cope quite successfully with 'a packet of cornflakes', 'a pound of raspberry jam' and 'a large piece of beef'. The butcher had a very hard time, because 'a chicken' or 'some sausages' were particularly difficult to say, but he had great patience, and took an especial interest in this eight-year-old deaf child who struggled so manfully to get her message across. She thought he was wonderful, and in one of her school books she wrote:

> The butcher's shop belongs to a butcher who is kind to me because I am just only a little girl. A butcher sells meat, pork, mutton and mince pies (!) It is my butcher's shop. It is in Baildon.

She was beginning to write little compositions of her own now. Another read:

> On Saturday I went to my dancing class with Mummy. My dancing class is downstairs. Mummy watched me dancing. On Sunday Philip was in the choir and Mummy and I were singing by it. In the afternoon I read a funny book about Mrs Pepperpot. She always shink like a pepper pot. And then I played with Philip. We played Grumpy [rummy] with cards. I like it very much. Before tea I went for a walk with my Daddy and Philip. I played in the playground and I rode a pretend horse. I drove a pretend ship. I slid. I was swinging. Then we went home for tea.

And again:

> On Saturday it was my birthday. I was eight years old. I had lots and lots of presents. I had a big drawing book, a long nightie, a blue case and a pair of pretty slippers from Mummy and Daddy.

I had four colour pens from Philip and a bottle of bubbles from Frances for my bath. I had a lovely birthday party. There was nine girls comming so there are twelve children in the party.

What she was writing tended to be formal and rather static, but it was basically accurate, and within the next year it was to take a great leap forward as she discovered books for herself, and her imagination was given a free rein.

In the meantime she expressed her imaginative self rather charmingly in the cards she drew for all the family. She adored art at school and won a Road Safety Competition during her eighth year. Frances was an accomplished designer of Christmas cards, and Judith copied her avidly, producing cards and drawings for every occasion: birthdays, Easter, Valentine's Day, Get Well, together with illustrations for the little stories she wrote; her figures romped across the pages bearing an individual stamp all of their own.

When she was seven she had been reading the Ladybird fairy story books with me: *The Sleeping Beauty, Red Riding Hood, Three Little Pigs*, etc. When she was eight she suddenly discovered Enid Blyton. She had been used to going with Daddy and the others to the library every week. The older two chose their books, and so did she. First picture books, then others I could read with her, and now at last she could read her own stories. And she did, anything and everything. Sometimes she'd finished the book before she arrived home. Even while she was getting dressed or undressed I would find an open Enid Blyton propped up on the chair beside her, while she absent-mindedly pulled her pants on. She may have risked pneumonia, but she certainly enlarged her horizons. And her own free writing really took off. From a stilted half-side she developed into writing three to four pages, retelling the story of the pantomime *Snow White*, recalling a visit to a Brownie Carol Service, to the ballet at Leeds, or making up her own very moral compositions about a rude boy or a silly girl. The Enid Blyton influence was to continue for two years, and her stories became peppered with exclamation marks, whole words in capitals and stuttering letters: ' "You HATEFUL JOAN!" shouted Jean. "I won't like you if you do this ONCE MORE! Joan why did you do this?" "B-b-because I-I-I w-was HUNGRY!" ' etc. but at last she was expressing what she really wanted to say. There were many situations she experienced when playing with other children that she needed to get out of her system, and instead of developing her own tantrums I think she fantasised about them on paper. It was an outlet, and a most valuable one.

During this year, 1968, I was studying very hard for my own Diploma as a Teacher of the Deaf, and I was able to attend a conference in Northern Ireland which was partly devoted to sound perception. It was fascinating to hear what was being done in the field of auditory training at St Michielsgestel in The Netherlands, and at Cabra in Ireland, and I went home with renewed energy, determined to work even harder on the rhythms of speech. We had always used nursery rhymes, but now I looked around for rhymes and jingles that were short enough for Judith to learn and to say with expression. We used the tape recorder a lot, so that I could play back what she was saying, and try and analyse what was wrong with it. She loved learning simple little poems and I found that, with the headphones, she could repeat them line by line with quite a lot of expression, and with varying intonation:

> I can walk on tip-toe
> Like a fairy I can go,
> I can *stamp*, so that you'll say
> An elephant is here today.

Or:

> Over in the meadow, where the stream runs blue,
> Lived an old mother fish and her little fishes too,
> *Swim* said the mother, we *swim* said the two,
> So they swam all the day where the stream runs blue.

We worked mainly on the rhythm, but because I now knew rather more about it, we worked also on the articulation. The adenoidal condition of her early childhood had meant that she was very slow in developing those consonants which demanded a free flow of breath. We worked on 'h', until she could put it into her reading aloud, automatically and less breathily. 'S' was still poor and 'sausages' were rendered as 'chauchaches' but she tried hard and could produce 's' correctly when reminded. The trouble was that she had so much to say when we talked together, that the words tumbled out in quick succession; 'm' became 'b', and 't' was still 'k', and I hesitated to stop her too often. We needed a free flow of speech or the rhythm would get lost, and it would become far less intelligible to the outsider. At the same time certain consonants were vital to intelligibility and 's' was one of them; she was cutting it too short, and we worked hard on this, because she needed a good long 's' in order to get combinations such as *star* and *swing* and *snake*. Fortunately she *wanted* to be able to say the poems properly, and she never seemed to mind practising. And it did her good in other ways as well, because it helped her to develop a good memory.

As a rule I don't think deaf children do have good memories, and Judith certainly didn't. She needed to rely on her eyes, to visualise something, before she could remember it. Frances and Philip helped her enormously by playing card games – Pelmanism in particular – and she sharpened her memory on this. It was easy of course for her to concentrate on cards, because she wasn't distracted by extraneous noise. Then, too, I made picture books for her, and photograph albums were a particular help, because without them she couldn't remember anything about the places we had been to, or the things we had seen. She frequently needed her memory jogging about all kinds of things, and Frances and Philip were surprised at how little she did in fact remember about the holidays we had had.

On the other hand her curiosity was intense. 'What's this for?' 'What's that for?' 'Why do you put your foot there?' (on the clutch in the car). She asked questions all day long, similar to the ones a hearing child would have asked at a much earlier stage.

She still played the piano, although she had to be coaxed into practising now! And she sang nursery rhymes all the way to school in the morning. She was nearly nine, and a hearing child would long have been past that stage, but she obviously got a great deal of pleasure from doing it, and so did I in listening to her. Fortunately we had a car of our own now, so it didn't really matter how much noise she made! She loved playing with the children who lived nearby but there were not very many in our immediate neighbourhood and there were times, naturally, when they didn't want her. Then she would get upset and come home saying, 'They won't play with me because I'm deaf.' Perhaps it was so, perhaps it was simply the squabbles all children go through, but we decided that she was probably ready for a wider companionship.

Chapter Eleven

FITTING IN WITH HEARING CHILDREN

During all the early years of her life, Judith's self-confidence had gradually grown. There had been occasional minor setbacks, but the discovery that sometimes children didn't want her because she was deaf was a major one. As long as she could play on a purely physical basis she was all right. She could swing as high as anybody on the swing. She could dance as well as they, because she learnt to watch the dancing teacher very, very closely and the other children too, and also she felt the vibrations through the floor. She could enjoy swimming. She played dolls, tea-parties and dressing up. She was good at cards and crayonning pictures. She had an additional ability to do things with a piano, that stood her in good stead, and if the local children thought her singing was peculiar, they were well-mannered enough not to mention it. But round about the age of nine, little girls have all sorts of secrets to share. And she was no good at that at all. The whispering in corners, the giggles, natural though it was, left her out in the cold; she wasn't one of them any more. *Her* communication had to be face to face in order to lip-read; the distortion of a sideways whispering was beyond her, and in despair she fled back to her books and her world of fantasy. Lack of confidence in this field meant lack of confidence in another: the dancing class. Here again, she withdrew as other children looked enquiringly at the hearing aid. There were longer gaps between the movement sessions; and the other children filled these in with chatting; this she felt she couldn't do, and she was obviously unhappy. And one day I was horrified to discover on a scrappy bit of paper in the playroom the statement, 'Judith has no real friends', obviously written by herself.

At school she was rather unlucky in that the children of her own age were mostly boys, and this mattered more at the age of nine than it had done when she was younger. She wanted to share her interests with girls, and there were not many available. Of the four deaf ones who were, the only one who lived near enough for local contact was quite a number of years older, and she and Judith had few interests in common. At this time Judith was fortunate, however, in having become friendly with deaf twins in Pudsey, and a deaf girl from Huddersfield, and many exchange visits went on between their homes. But it was not easy. The children were too young at this stage to be able to make complicated bus journeys by themselves, and much depended on the goodwill of parents. The parents of the deaf are seldom lacking in this respect, and a great deal of ferrying backwards and forwards went on to parties, to swimming baths, to pantomimes, or just simply to play for the day, and quite often to stay for the night. It was exhausting, but it was worth it; the children delighted in each other's company.

Nevertheless, Judith, because she had been brought up within a hearing environment, wanted desperately to fit into it. *Could* she manage in a normal school? Or would she sink if we tried it? To move from a class of 10 deaf children into one with 30-plus hearing ones, was obviously too big a jump. Miss B herself, the Head of the Bradford School for the Deaf, suggested that Judith might try the preparatory department of the girls' grammar school. It would mean paying for her, but a small legacy had been left for her education by a very dear aunt, and we resolved to use it in this way. A further factor in deciding to do this, was that Judith had by now outstripped her peers in what she could achieve at school and had arrived in my own class. As I had at this time a class of five very deaf boys, of 15–16, plus five very deaf girls of the same age, plus the deaf twins who were only 12, the addition of Judith, not yet 10, was an impossible situation. It was wrong for her, it was wrong for the class, and it was an embarrassment to me.

Judith was seen by an educational psychologist and was given an IQ test. Unlike most deaf children, because her language skills were so good, she scored almost as highly on the verbal test as she did on the performance. Contact was made with the Head of the grammar school, and Judith was seen by the Head of the preparatory department. While obviously being eager to help she found it difficult to understand Judith's speech and was also worried on other counts. How would Judith react to instructions if she couldn't hear them, especially in games? How could she cope with safety precautions in science lessons? The fears were natural, but I endeavoured to dispel them. Judith was *used* to managing. She had quick reactions. She would watch the others very closely, and she was a most obedient child. I didn't think they would have much difficulty in that respect. What worried me far more was how the other children would react to her. After a useful and lengthy discussion, it was suggested that perhaps Judith could be given a six weeks trial, and for a week I agonised over whether this was going to take place.

In the meantime we worked hard on her speech. I had neglected it for some months. She had been making such progress at school, and I had been so involved with my own deaf class, and with home commitments, that other things had crowded it out, and for almost six months we had done very little articulation practice. Six months back, in August 1969, she had at last achieved a 't', and she was so thrilled by the achievement that we had had to keep practising all through the day. She wouldn't do it without the headphones on; she said she needed them to hear anything and so we recited endlessly 'tea' and 'table' and 'tar', leading on to 'boat' and 'went' and 'bottle'.

By April 1970, when she was nine and a half, she could achieve all the sounds of speech, and she would put them in whenever we worked together on the ATU, delighting in reciting 'The Owl and the Pussycat' or 'There are Hundreds of Numbers' – but the minute she was back playing with her friends, or talking to the family, she would forget all about the consonants. I resolved to be much tougher and started pulling her up about her speech. I didn't like doing this, and I tried to choose my moments carefully, but if she were going out to mix with hearing children the quality of her speech would be all-important.

After a week's anxious waiting, we heard that Judith had been accepted for a trial period at Lady Royd and was to start almost immediately. I delivered her to the school two days later. There was a confident 'Good morning' on Judith's behalf, and she disappeared immediately in the wake of the Head. I went on to my own job and wondered throughout the day how she would fare. I need not have worried! She came home on the school bus absolutely bursting with conversation, the names of the girls, the subjects she was doing, what they did at playtime, and at dinner, in gym and at games and outside. She was put at first with children two years younger, but within a week she was moved up into a class of her own age. They accepted her from the first and were exceedingly kind to her. I felt that someone, somewhere, had done a very good public relations job behind the scenes, and I was eternally grateful.

For the first week she enquired constantly, 'Has anyone at my old school asked about me?' but by the end of a month she was obviously far more concerned with 'my new school' and quite definitely wanted to stay. It was lucky that they decided to extend her trial period for another term, for Judith would have been heartbroken if they had rejected her. Her confidence increased enormously. She made no bones about travelling on the bus and paying for herself, nor did she hesitate to chatter to her companions on the way home. Her lip-reading progressed too. She began to pay much more attention to the TV – perhaps because the other children referred to it and she wanted to be in the swim. But it was very evident just how little she *did* hear. With the most powerful amplification available through the headphones – 135dB (i.e. greater than the noise made by pneumatic drills, rock bands, etc) – she could distinguish between the vowel sounds to some extent, but she could not make out a single word. She could, however, distinguish between lines of nursery rhymes purely by rhythm, e.g. 'Baa, Baa, Black Sheep' from 'See-Saw, Margery Daw'. And similarly she could hear the difference between 'How *old* are you?' and 'Where do you *live*?' because she had been listening to these phrases for almost eight years. I used to cover up my mouth so that there was no possibility of lip-reading, when I wanted to test her in this way. Later on, of course, when she was older, I could get her to turn her back so that she couldn't get any clues whatsoever from the rest of my face. But we didn't do this kind of testing too often. It was too disheartening. 'Thirty-seven' could just as easily be 'forty-seven' by her reckoning, 'thin' could be 'sun', 'sheep' could be 'feet' and 'ball' could be 'four'. It served no useful purpose, except possibly to remind me yet again just how little she *did* hear and how totally dependent on lip-reading she was.

When she got her first report from Lady Royd it was evident just how happy she was. Socially the experiment had done her the world of good. She had a pleasant nature and mixed readily with anyone who was willing to accept her, and she was delighted to receive invitations to the parties of two of her new-found friends. Academically, although she had achieved quite a high mark in English, there were signs that she was finding the work difficult. 'Sometimes her vocabulary has not been sufficient to cope with the passages concerned', 'In discussions she has difficulty in keeping pace with the form', 'At times in lessons she has been unable to follow the development of ideas', were typical comments. We wondered what the future might bring.

Chapter Twelve

WIDENING HORIZONS

In the meantime Judith continued to fit into family life at home and to benefit from it. She was 10 now. Her brother was 13 and her sister 15. They had their own friends and interests, but they still continued to make time to play with her and to talk to her. Pelmanism and Ludo had developed into Monopoly and Pit – the latter a game we encouraged as much as possible, so as to make the most use of her voice. Many a time, as I passed between kitchen and dining-room, I would hear the frantic shouts of 'wheat' or 'barley' issuing from the playroom, and know that the corn market was functioning again. She introduced these games to other children who came to play, and had a large stock of card games, including several varieties of patience to teach them as well.

Frances and Philip had their own friends, but this too enlarged Judith's horizons. Philip's friends in particular quite often came to the house, and once the problem had been explained to them, they were willing to include her in their interests whenever practicable. She was invited to share in N's bonfire or to admire R's new bicycle, and all her life she continued to regard them as *her* friends too, and to enquire for years afterwards as to what they were doing now.

Frances added a new dimension when she began taking part in foreign exchanges and French girls came to stay. With Judith's imperfect speech it was difficult for the foreigners to follow what she said, and she, on her part, found it difficult to follow them, but they widened her outlook and increased her interest in foreign countries. Our caravan had by now ventured abroad, to Brittany in 1968, and to Belgium, France and Luxemburg in 1970, the tenth year of her life. All this Judith revelled in. The food was difficult at first, as she tended to be conservative in her eating habits, but the crêpes and frites of Brittany were an immediate success, and she gradually learnt to accept the strange tastes of foreign countries. This apart, the new sights and sounds enchanted her. She tripped into French swimming baths with Frances and Philip, she marvelled at the Grottes de Hans, she floated on Luxemburg rivers and laughed at my fears of French cable cars. She helped to carry home French bread, and shop in French markets, and she thoroughly enjoyed the two exciting ferry trips. The only things that meant little to her were the castles and museums, the cathedrals and the stately homes, for she had no sense of history. The gaps in a deaf child's education are serious ones. At her deaf school, history was only absorbed incidentally, because there was no time for everything. Hence she had never been able to enjoy books with an historical flavour, and so the gap grew ever wider. She was bored with the historical monuments around her, and was to be so for years, until a friend of her own shamed her into taking an interest.

At home she continued to play the piano. She had changed teachers now, but got on equally well with Mrs M, the elderly lady who taught her. Her playing was almost on a par with hearing children of the same age, and she was entered with them for the annual concerts in 1970 and 1971. By now she could play a simple piece of Mozart, and it was only when she had finished, that her teacher, proud of her achievement, explained to the audience that she was profoundly deaf.

She was gradually acquiring greater confidence with strangers, and she coped well now with unfamiliar situations. This year it became obvious that her eyes needed testing, but she managed this quite well, giving her responses clearly and composedly. And then a verruca necessitated a visit to hospital for an operation, but she made no fuss about this, nor about the discomfort before and afterwards. Physical pain she made light of; perhaps it is insignificant compared to loss of hearing. By the time she was 10 she liked to travel further on her own; she was always energetic and she needed to get out more. I felt that her handicap made her particularly vulnerable where strangers were concerned: she could not hear if anyone were to approach her from behind, and the woods and moors were lonely. We decided that perhaps a dog would be a good idea for protection and also for companionship. When she was five and a half she had had a guinea pig of her own but it had not lived long. When she was nine and a half she had written in her school book:

> Frances has a pet and it is a dear little girl rabbit, about five years old. The rabbit is white all over and it lives in a big hutch in our shed. Philip, once, had some hamsters and a mouse, but they are all dead a long time ago. I have a pet goldfish, which I have to feed every night before I go to bed. But I wish that I had a pet that could breathe on air, so that I could play with it and cuddle it, like lucky Frances does to her rabbit! I love that rabbit. It is called Silver.

The composition had been about 'My Family' but the major part of it was this section on the rabbit, and it was obvious that she really cared quite deeply. We decided that for once, for her 10th birthday, she should have a more expensive present than usual, and Snow Annaliese of Carwood came on the scene, a most beautiful Samoyed.

We chose a Samoyed, partly because I am allergic to hair, and the Samoyed is woolly, but also because it is a tribal dog, and I knew that Frances and Philip would have to help her to look after it. And so it proved. Philip, the handyman, made a sleeping box and a chicken-wire pen in the garden, and we collected Lisa on our way back from the Continent, for the kennels were at Northampton. She was small and white and woolly and very, very nervous. On the journey up to Yorkshire she lay peaceably enough across the children's knees in the back of the car, but she took an instant dislike to her bed in the porch and bounded upstairs to lie quivering under my bed. She had to be fetched down again and again, and Judith had to learn to be firm with her and yet to give her the affection and reassurance she needed. Lisa required a great deal of brushing, and the others helped her at this, and also to control her when she went for walks, for she was a sled dog and had powerful neck muscles. As she was Kennel Club registered we experimented with showing her at the local dog shows, but this was a disaster. Lisa did not consider that posing to order was her scene at all, and we decided that the time involved in getting her ready was more than we could afford in any case. Judith, Philip and I went to training classes together every week but although Lisa became amenable to kerb drill she never really lost her habit of straining at the leash, for it was too deeply ingrained within her. That apart, however, she became a valuable addition to the family and was to stay with us for 11 years. She proved a focal point of interest, for she was very beautiful, and this was to prove most useful. People often stopped to admire her, conversations were started, and Judith was encouraged to be more outgoing.

Judith continued to enjoy her new school and to delight in the fresh playmates she had found. Eight came to her 10th birthday party, and we wondered how best to use the time so that neither they, nor Judith, were at a disadvantage. In the end my husband took them swimming, where deafness is no handicap, and they had a truly riotous time. Then, after tea, Frances and Philip organised games for them at home.

Judith was very happy indeed at Lady Royd. She seemed to be coping with the work, she undoubtedly was benefiting from the social contact with the other children, and we were delighted with the progress she had made. It was therefore a most unpleasant shock when, as a result of a discussion between the Heads of the two schools Judith had attended, we were told that they did not feel she could continue in normal education. Her reports had been largely non-committal. 'Works with interest, reads with understanding, makes a steady effort, plans her work carefully', and none of these revealed the difficulties she had in fact been experiencing. We knew that she was bright, and had thought she was coping and being stretched. Her third report, when she had been at Lady Royd for a year, revealed that this was not, in fact, so. She was falling well below the standard she should have reached. Whereas the top mark in arithmetic was 75 per cent, she was getting 38 per cent. It was the same in science, geography and history; and even in English, her best subject, she was well down, in comparison with the rest of the pupils. She was obviously not going to be able to pass from the preparatory department into the main school at the age of 11; discussions in the classroom would always be beyond her.

This was a bitter blow. Judith was well integrated into the local community by now. She exchanged continual visits with her hearing friends, she was now a member of the local Brownie pack and had made new contacts there, she had her piano lessons, and had added a weekly skating lesson, she had her beloved dog, and above all she had the love and support of her extended family – grandparents, uncles, aunts, cousins – every single one of whom had contributed to her sense of security. How would she fare if all this were swept away? If the widening horizons open to her from a secure home base, were to be replaced by the more restricted ones of a deaf boarding school, the only alternative. Would the greater academic progress she might make be worth the loss of social contact? Would her speech deteriorate if she were placed all day long only with other deaf children? Would she be lonely in the deaf school's holidays which, from the necessity of cramming as much as possible into the academic year, were arranged differently. Instead of the normal three school terms, there were four; she came home towards the end of June and went back in August. Would she ever reknit the ties she was about to break? We wondered and we agonised, as the time approached for a decision to be made.

Chapter Thirteen

A DIFFICULT DECISION

The decision to send Judith away to school was the most difficult of all to make. How does one balance intellectual fulfilment against social integration? How can one tell which is going to benefit one's child the most? How does one know in fact that either will be achieved? I had known of the Mary Hare School at Newbury for many years. I had listened to its pupils speaking on TV in the 1960s and I had not been able to understand what they said. On a more encouraging note I had attended a professional meeting there in 1965 when Judith was four and a half. I knew what a wonderful situation the school had. I knew of its glorious grounds, its impressive hall and well-equipped classrooms, and I had heard of its reputation. But to send an 11-year-old child there for six or seven years of its life; to have only one month out of 12 to rediscover her in the holidays! To break the knot that held her, for we had an excellent relationship. Deaf children, as a rule, are honest and forthright. For 11 years she and I had exchanged our confidences, and I did feel exceptionally close to her. And yet, perhaps, the time had come to break that knot. She had grown in confidence. I knew that she had the ability to cope in unknown situations, she had proved that numerous times. Gradually, as the autumn wore on, I came to accept the necessity for her going away, and it was decided that she should sit the entrance examination in January 1971.

Now came the task of convincing Judith herself. She was unbelievably happy amongst her hearing friends, and had hoped to move with them into the senior school. How would she react? Was she mature enough to make her own decision? No, we decided, not at 10 years old. We began to make contact with other Mary Hare children in the area. I knew of two Bradford children less deaf than Judith, who had gone to this school. We spoke to their parents. We exchanged several visits with another family from Leeds who were hoping their child might go there too. Judith started taking an interest, and my own fears began to disappear. In due course Judith sat the entrance examination for the Mary Hare School. She sat under another teacher's supervision of course, and I never knew what she had written, but she came home strained and tired, and missed her Brownie Pack for that week. 1971 was the year of the postal strike, and so my husband and I arranged to deliver the papers of the three local Mary Hare candidates personally. This was an excellent opportunity for my husband to visit the school, and for myself to see it for the second time. We were both very impressed.

In March came the news that Judith had been accepted for interview, and again she and I travelled to Newbury. This time I left her at the door for a whole day of tests and interviews. She was very wound up when I collected her at 3 p.m., but unable to explain very much about what had happened, and so we settled down to await results.

In the meantime I wrote to the Head of the Bradford Girls' Grammar School (Miss B) explaining that if a place were offered at Mary Hare 'it would probably be unfair to Judith's ultimate good if we were to refuse'. I stated, however, that I was far from happy about certain aspects, namely the difference in the holiday dates, the breaking of the contact with the hearing world, and the possible deterioration of speech. Miss B was most helpful. It was arranged that Judith should sit the entrance examination for Bradford Girls' Grammar School (at which she did in fact reach the qualifying standard) and she was to be allowed to go into the Bradford Girls' Grammar School in July and October to do largely practical subjects, but, most importantly, to renew all her contacts with her hearing friends. The knowledge that she did not have to lose these entirely, helped Judith to accept the inevitable, and she approached her forthcoming separation with good grace.

One girl in particular from Lady Royd had become a very real friend, so much so that in the absence abroad of the older children we took this girl with us on holiday in the summer. The acceptance of each other by the two Judiths was total; they swam, walked, shopped, explored and in wet weather played innumerable card games together. And always they chatted. Thus the pattern was set for years to come; the outgoing spirit of Judith B was to be of inestimable value in encouraging the flow of conversation from Judith S.

It was on this holiday, however, that disaster nearly struck, and the dangers of deafness were reinforced very strongly. The girls had each acquired a new and shining beach ball, their pride and joy. They played with them on the beach all the time, but the winds on the Northumberland coast can get up suddenly. A gust caught our daughter's ball and carried it into the waves. Shrieking with merriment she gaily plunged after it. She knew she could swim, and she was utterly fearless. Within two minutes she was fast disappearing in pursuit of the brightly coloured ball which floated relentlessly on. We stood aghast, knowing we could not call her back; knowing determination would carry her on and on. And then we shouted, all of us, trying to attract the attention of the only swimmer who was anywhere near her. Mercifully he sized up the situation quickly and managed to overhaul her. We shouted to him to turn her to face the shore, and then we were able to pantomime to her that she should come back at once and let the ball go. She cried for the loss of the beach ball, but one look at our horror-stricken faces made her realise just how anxious we had been. There were no more beach balls that holiday.

A happier event of that year was our participation in 'Ask the Family'. We had passed a preliminary Yorkshire round, and in June we were invited up to London to take part in the next heat. Naturally Judith went too. She enjoyed all the sight-seeing we were enabled to do first – the BBC were very generous and entertained us for the whole weekend – and so she saw Trafalgar Square and Hyde Park, the Post Office Tower and Madame Tussauds; and she was probably the only one who thoroughly enjoyed her lunch on the following day, *we* were all far too nervous! For the recording itself she was allowed to sit up in the box with the technicians, and if she couldn't decipher question and answer at least she had a grandstand view and the opportunity of meeting Robert Robinson. Her main comments afterwards concerned our appearance. Well, yes, she had enjoyed watching us all – 'But you looked awfully bright, Mum', a reference to my shocking pink, and a suitably deflating one!

The time of her departure for boarding school was now drawing very near. A trunk was bought, her clothes were sorted out, and her 11th birthday party was forwarded by two months so that she should have the company of hearing friends. The format of this was as before: swimming, which deaf and hearing children could all participate in together, and specially chosen games where the deaf children would be at no disadvantage. Riotously they tore around the garden pursuing a car-race game; companionably they giggled together over the individualistic Beetles which some of them drew. It was a success, and it proved convincingly that with give and take on both sides the hearing child could accept the deaf one for what really mattered: the personality behind the handicap.

The following day, perhaps inevitably, reaction set in. Judith was lost and disconsolate, and in an attempt to stave off the blues we went shopping together, looking for the items she still needed for boarding school. We had a final family holiday together in Scotland, where she was diverted by the two extra French children we had with us, and then in mid-August came the moment I had been dreading, her departure for Newbury. We took her down, we saw the new classroom, we left her in her new surroundings and we returned to a house that seemed curiously empty. The piano stood silent, her ATU still sitting upon it. Her bedroom, piled high with books, was unnaturally tidy. Her joyous spirit was missing from the house, and my own life seemed strangely hollow.

Chapter Fourteen

BOARDING SCHOOL

But the young are ever resilient. Her first letters, in August 1971, reflected her interest and enthusiasm for the new life that lay ahead of her.

Dear Everybody,

I got both letters from Mummy on Saturday at breakfast. We had Rice Krispies and sausages for breakfast and mince, cabbage and potatoes and jam tart for dinner on Saturday.

It is true the suppers are very good here – breakfasts etc. are rather small but supper's the best of all.

There are six girls and four boys in my class – 1A – and seven girls in my dormitory.

I'm writing in Jane's pen because Oh dear I've lost the pen Helen gave me at my party! I don't really think I'll find it at all.

I'm in House Beverley. I went swimming on Saturday morning. It was fine! I don't know if I'm playing tennis or hockey yet.

Can you send some 3p stamps and also more envelopes as I've used them all?

Love to Lisa.

Judith

She wrote faithfully every week – indeed she had to, because Monday morning at school was 'letters home' time – and thus began a long series of correspondence which was to keep us very much in touch with all her activities and thoughts. She was too deaf to use even the adapted telephone which Mary Hare provided, and so she poured out her thoughts, her opinions and her descriptions of her new life on to reams and reams of writing paper:

> Dear Family,
>
> I'm still enjoying myself here. I had a terrible fall a few days ago. I was on my way swimming and I rounded a corner of the pool and then I slipped and bumped my mouth. I put my hand on my mouth and when I looked at my hand I found that it was covered with blood and then (I hope you don't mind) I cried. I got up and staggered on and then a teacher spotted me and helped me to wipe my mouth. I found that, when I jumped in the water, I felt as strong as if it had never happened and I did one length breast stroke very quickly and strongly, though I do it very slowly and weakly usually. I found that my upper lip had swelled and everybody said I looked funny and I thought so too. But the swelling has gone now but there is a little scratch at the top of my mouth. In the middle of the night I went to the loo in my sleep in my bed!
>
> Lots of love,
>
> Judith
>
> X   X   X   X   X   X
>
> Mum Dad Frances Philip Lisa Goldie
>
> I hope Lisa and Goldie are alright. I miss you really.

She remained most firmly attached to everyone and everything at home. She asked repeated questions as to their welfare, and when the time of our first visit drew near, she obviously longed for the companionship of her dog:

> Dear All,
>
> I wish Lisa could come with you because I miss her as much as well as all of you and also I want everybody to see her. Can't you try? You can leave her can't you for a few hours in the car?
>
> It is funny about Lisa jumping in the canal in Chester and coming out like a drowned rat! . . .
>
> What did you mean about 'P.S. Sorry Daddy says no Lisa this time?' Does it mean that Lisa can't come, oh I do hope not, I do hope that Lisa can come!

For various reasons it was impossible to take Lisa on this occasion. We were due at the Mary Hare Speech Day on 1 October and we set off very early with the caravan, trundling terribly slowly down the M1. I was worried lest we should be late, particularly as this was a rather special occasion; Judith, being the youngest child at school, had been selected to present a brooch to Princess Margaret, the patron. We left the caravan at Newport Pagnell, changed hurriedly, and drove on to Newbury. Mercifully we were in time. Judith managed to say her few words quite clearly, and, contrary to her expectations, she did not fall down the steps afterwards!

'This is for you' – a presentation to Princess Margaret (photo reproduced with the permission of the *Evening Post*, Reading)

We took Judith back with us to the caravan site and we had the weekend together visiting the Woburn Abbey Game Reserve, looking at all her birthday presents and above all catching up with all the news. Photos needed to be exchanged, letters from friends read, questions asked and answered. It was wonderful to see her again, and very soon it was as if she had never been away. A weekend is all too short, however. On the Sunday afternoon we took her back to school and set off on the long journey home. We left her in tears, her slight figure in its green uniform standing in the portico of the large country mansion. My heart ached, and I wondered, not for the first time, whether this perpetual separation and reunification would prove in the end to be worth all the distress it caused at the time.

In October the school had a fortnight's holiday, one week of which coincided with my own half-term. For this, I resolved to take her away. She was still of an age to travel cheaply and I decided on a mini-cruise to Norway. I wrote to ask her opinion and the response was immediate: 'Yes I would *love* to go to Norway – I don't believe it at all! Suppose there was a storm at sea!' Prophetic words!

We set off from Newcastle one Saturday afternoon; within an hour I was feeling decidedly queasy. I staggered up to the dining saloon for the evening meal, but the sight of all that luscious food was to prove too much; poor Judith had to be left to fend for herself while I crawled back to my bunk below. And that was to be the pattern for four out of our seven days. The voyage home was even rougher. I lay prostrated in the lower bunk, hardly able to lift my head from the pillow, while she peered merrily down at me from the top bunk, drew me pictures to cheer me up, and wrote me funny messages. Every few hours she disappeared up on deck to get some air or to partake of the magnificent Norwegian buffets. She was completely on her own; I had been taken ill almost immediately, and we had had no time to contact fellow passengers. She was just eleven, and she coped admirably. Sandwiched into the middle of all the sea-sickness we had three glorious days together exploring Oslo, and she showed a great interest in the Viking museums and in the Kontiki, in the folk museum on Bygdby and in the Vigeland Sculptor park. There were endless things to see, to explain and to talk about, and for me there was the delightful rediscovery of a charming companion.

The holiday soon passed, and the remaining week was more difficult to arrange. I was fully occupied with my own job, my husband was also working, and Frances and Philip were at school. As we had arranged, Judith went for two full days into the girls' grammar school. She enjoyed this at first. She caught up on her hearing friends' news, she joined them in practical activities, and she was able to compare what they were doing with her own new school. On two other days, she went into my school with me. I felt this was harder, for it was now a year and a half since she had left. But there were many people there whom she knew and she had much to talk about. In the evenings, after school, she saw all her relations, went out with her grandparents or her godmother and took up the threads with her local friends, who all came for tea one day after the other.

It was a successful fortnight and I began to feel that perhaps she *could* keep a foot in both camps – the deaf world and the hearing. She came home again at Christmas, this time travelling with a party to Leeds, and being met there by my husband. She was still cheerful, bubbling over with things to tell us and she slotted back easily into our home commitments. It was a strange Christmas, for my mother was ill, and Christmas dinner was eaten in her bedroom by all of us, but Judith did her share, never grumbling at the inconvenience this caused, at staggering down the road with trays of food, or at my own frequent absences on nursing duties. In the time available we saw all her other cousins at the Boxing Day party, took her to *Toad of Toad Hall* with her deaf friends, went swimming with others, shopped at the sales, and whenever possible I tried to renew her lessons on the ATU. Her speech had not deteriorated, as we had feared, but neither had it improved, and she was in fact exactly at the point where we had broken off six months before. She could remember 't' and 's' when reminded, but 'sh', 'j' and 'ch' were very difficult for her.

As the time approached for her return she gradually became quieter and more and more weepy, and this was to be the pattern all through her schooldays. The last day or two of the holidays were always agony to get through, and it was necessary to keep her occupied all the time, and preferably to reserve the best treats until last. It was becoming much more noticeable too, that the occasions when the family were all together were the occasions when she felt her deafness the most. She could not follow the quick-fire exchange of information, the jokes, the repartee, and she felt terribly left out. While she was little, this family gossip was less important. She could leave it to her elders and retire to play games, but now she wanted to know what everyone was saying; she needed to be included, and it was very hard to feel she was only on the outskirts. This was to happen on every festive occasion throughout her life.

When she was away she obviously missed her family very much and her letters contained phrases such as: 'I am sorry I cried, but you see I felt homesick again when you were just leaving.' 'Please can you write to me, Frances or Philip, PLEASE, PLEASE.' 'So please can you tell me how Granny is?' She sent kisses for everyone and paw-marks and licking-tongues for Lisa, and she wrote copious details of every film that was seen and every match that was played. Weekends at school she found intensely boring. She was not a sportsman and found that Saturdays and Sundays dragged.

Half-term visits she looked forward to most eagerly. It was too far to fetch her home for a mere weekend, and so instead we travelled to her, collecting her from school and taking her with us to visit friends and relations in the south of England. The extent of her interest in her cousins' activities was boundless. She borrowed Carol's books, she wanted to see Wendy's new house, she watched while Heather played the cello. She could not have heard much of the latter, but it was a new experience to see a bow drawn across strings, and therefore it was worth watching. And her cousins for their part tried to make her brief stay a happy one.

All too soon she had to be delivered back to Newbury and the letters resumed: 'Guess what – the pool is broken yet *again*. AGAIN. It's not fair, NOT FAIR at all.' 'I was goalkeeper last week and it was AWFULLY BORING. Nothing to do as the ball was at the other side of the pitch. Once I was centre half and it was very exciting.' 'I didn't play in the netball matches of course, but I did stand on the sides and cheer.'

When it came to athletics in the summer term she wrote eagerly of the others' achievements – and somewhat pathetically of her own: 'I can jump in High Jump no higher than three feet. Not very good really. Last Monday my time for the hundred metres was only 17.9. I'm terrible at javelin too!! [with an amusing illustration!] I think the only thing I like and can do is SWIMMING!!' Obviously, at boarding school, prowess in sports counted for a good deal, but at least she had the release of being able to write down her failings and disappointments.

Sometimes there were problems: 'Do you know what? I went shopping and ate a toffee. I felt something hard in my mouth, so I took it out and discovered that it was a FILLING! What can I do about it? . . .'

And later: 'My tooth doesn't hurt so much now, as I'm used to it.'

She admitted to weeping when her new watch was broken, and she had a long wait before it was mended. And inevitably there were times when she broke things (she was rather clumsy) and had to forfeit her pocket money to pay for them, or she lost some of her property.

In the main, however, her letters were cheerful, full of details as to what she had made in cookery, what they were rehearsing for the Talent Contest, how they had been to see *Julius Caesar*, which films they had watched, and the weekend walks and how they 'had enjoyed paddling in puddles'.

She seized eagerly on the comic bits: 'Last Tuesday we had cookery. We were getting things ready when suddenly, in a bag of flour, we found two sweet mice! But Mrs C didn't approve of them and demanded that the men should kill them. Then we found another mouse in the pantry. We never caught it, so probably it is in its hole. The best cookery lesson ever!'

And: 'Once a boy, Paul, put a worm in Jane's dress! and she screamed! For one whole minute the worm wriggled about then fell out! Ooh it was terrible! She can't bear worms (and neither can I!).'

She revelled in anything that was a change from the ordinary routine, and particularly in secret things: 'I had a great time looking for tunnels and little hidey holes which were used during the war', and, 'Last night everybody in our dormitory played about, switching on and off the light, rolling over on our beds and fighting.' 'On Friday night most of the first form girls had a MIDNIGHT FEAST in the basement of the cellar. It was good fun! We weren't caught. Please don't tell on us!' She obviously felt herself to be one of the gang. Childish things were being outgrown. 'I do not want the dolls' things in the playroom any more. Please could you do something about it?'

Whether to wear socks or tights, how to rearrange her hairstyle, what she thought of the summer uniform, were becoming questions of the hour, because those were the things the other girls were interested in. She was very conscious of the fact that she would soon be twelve, and a second former, and she was obviously looking forward to further years at her new school.

Everything and everybody is okay here – no weeping.

P.S. I have broken no more pots!

P.P.S. I can hardly wait til the end of term! This Friday is the last time I go shopping, have a bath in the first form!

P.P.P.S. Sorry if I make a few mistakes in this letter but nobody has inspected it as they're busy with exams, exams, exams!

P.P.P.P.S. Did you have a nice 'Father's Day'?

Because she wrote so fully of her own activities, and enquired so voraciously about ours, we did not feel that we were ever really out of touch. Once she tried to phone – quite a few of the other girls could manage this – but for us it was a disaster; we could not hear what she said, and as she could not even tell whether there was a voice there or not, she made no more attempts for many years. We made one visit to Newbury in the summer term, for Sports Day, but she was confined to sick bay with German measles, and all we could do was to play card games with her in turn while one of us reported on the activities outside.

At the beginning of July she came home for the summer, bearing with her a report that showed her to have 'maintained a high position' in most subjects and particularly in English which was 'outstanding for such a deaf girl'. Not for the first time I blessed our early conversations and all that reading she had done.

Chapter Fifteen

KEEPING IN TOUCH

That year, 1972, we had sold the caravan. It was becoming expensive to transport it abroad because of new ferry rates, and we felt that all three children were of ages – 17, 15 and 12 – to benefit from Continental contacts. We went instead into a gîte in Switzerland. For Judith this brought other benefits. On caravan sites we had found that Europeans, for the most part, set up barriers around their own little patch, to maintain their privacy. Sometimes these barriers were physical – and neat little white fences went up enclosing the dog, the cat, the geraniums and even the canary – sometimes they were merely psychological, but the effect was the same. Privacy was the aim, and isolation was achieved. Perhaps if one is to be there for a month this is very necessary! A gîte was very different. Our chalet, in true Swiss style, had been divided into three layers. All three sections mingled freely in the garden after chores were done. Judith became very friendly with two Dutch children – Manuela and Gilbert – and played many games of table tennis with them in the garden. She joined them also for swimming in the nearest pool, and we all went together to enjoy the fireworks on 1 August, the Swiss National Day. Another contact had been made, another address was written down for her.

How she kept all this correspondence going was a miracle, but she did, and it meant that when she returned at Christmas she could take up the threads immediately with each and every one of her friends. There were three groups – the deaf friends, the Lady Royd friends and the local friends. Somehow or other a visit to each one had to be arranged, both at their house and at ours, and for this my husband became her invaluable secretary. He would telephone them all, with Judith standing by his side to corroborate details, and he was endlessly patient, acting as interpreter throughout and passing on the vital messages.

Meanwhile her life at school continued. Her second-year letters were fuller than those of the first year but the mixture was very much as before: 'Hi, how are you? I hope you're not missing me too much. I enjoyed every minute of my hols, I really did . . . .' 'My bath and hairwash is now Monday and Thursday. What a nuisance! Two hairwashes in one week! And what a waste of shampoo!'

There were the same details of every sporting event in which her friends were concerned, and the inevitable comments on films – these were the highlight of the weekend and to be deprived of them was a severe penalty: 'At 10 p.m. the first formers switched the light on, and we joined in their playing about. But a matron found out, and we had to miss the film on Saturday. It was *Pride and Prejudice* but V couldn't understand it anyway so it was alright.'

Where Eagles Dare she found 'terribly good' because there were 'bombs, snow, blood, murders and daring things', but on the other hand in *Chisum*, 'there was fighting of course, but there was rather a lot of talking, so the film was a bit boring.' *Pollyanna*, *Jane Eyre* and *The Incredible Journey* met with her approval. Of the last she wrote: 'It was a very good and sad film. Most of the second form girls cried (including me)', and, somewhat scornfully: 'V and A cried, of course. (I think they cry every film here!)'

There were occasional flashes of homesickness: 'Has it been snowing up in beloved Yorkshire?' and continual references to the family: 'I'm not so pleased that Philip will be going off to Greece before I come home. . . .' 'And what would Daddy like for his birthday? Something for his garden, from a mower to a little daisy?'

Drawings embellished all her letters – of how a tree fell on the school swimming bath, of the first pizza she had ever made, and the exploding oven, of collages of monsters made in art, of trampolining in the gym, of what she thought Philip's glasses might look like, and of the new clothes she thought he ought to buy with his allowance.

As usual, she made light of what to us was hair-raising: 'Oh yes, I nearly got run over! You see there was a little passage-way from the ring [at a show] and I crossed it quickly just before two horses pulling a carriage came along. And two ladies were crossing it too. One just escaped by a few inches, but the other was almost trampled by the horses. The carriage went over the lady like this [drawing]. V screamed – that made me frightened.'

Attitudes from the others were soon caught. Church became 'a waste of time', she couldn't understand it anyway, and it became simply 'boring old church'. Weekends still dragged: 'Please bring my tapistry down if you happen to see it, also please, please may I borrow one or two very old tennis balls because I get fed up with skipping sometimes.'

Five firm friends at Mary Hare

Now she had friends at school, however, she could occasionally spend weekends with them if they lived near enough, and she looked forward to this eagerly. She tried hard to follow her friends' interests, and if pop records meant little to her, she did at least keep abreast of her friends' tastes.

Our half-term trips to the school continued, and during the February ones we were able to see the school in session. This we found invaluable and worth the disruption it must have caused to the school and even the nail-biting it must have occasioned the staff! Without these visits we should have felt much more cut-off from the school and all it was trying to do.

For the main holidays Judith travelled home and back by train. There were occasional mishaps. Once, when I was late in meeting her at Bradford, I found her in tears, for she had inadvertently handed in the return half of her ticket. It had gone in the bag with hundreds of others, the porter couldn't understand her, and she didn't know what to do. But in the main such misunderstandings were rare.

In the summer of 1973, Judith still went in to the grammar school for part of July, and still attended the deaf school with me, but it was becoming obvious that as her own school workload increased, so she needed to spend the six weeks of summer relaxing, not in a school environment, and the following year we decided to take this up with the Head of Mary Hare. In the meantime, relations and friends were exceedingly good at 'minding' her. She was almost 13, but we did not like leaving her alone all day in an empty house. She was too vulnerable if strangers came, she could not telephone, and if an accident were to happen we should never have forgiven ourselves.

This summer we had our last holiday all together as a family. We rented a cottage at Drumore and the children rediscovered each other. The only blot on the horizon was when Judith lost Lisa, on a very wet day. A bedraggled dog arrived back at the cottage on her own and a search had to be put in hand for the missing owner! But after an initial panic Judith was eventually located, and poor Lisa suitably chastised. It was a happy summer, and it was good to feel that in spite of their widely diverging interests the children could still enjoy each others' company and that Judith's deafness made no difference.

Chapter Sixteen

THE TEENAGER

For the next two years, between 13 and 15, Judith was to continue to enjoy her boarding school. There were occasional traces of homesickness: 'This morning, when Matron woke me up, I was dreaming that I was at home and that Mum was just waking me up and Lisa trying to put her nose through my arm. I wish it was true!'

And undoubtedly her mind, both waking and sleeping, went back often to the life she had left behind: 'Remembrance Sunday – did you be silent for two minutes at 11 a.m.? We did. Where were you? At church? In bed? Cooking the dinner? Talking to Lisa? or what?'

She thought constantly of the family: 'Frances is going to University – I wonder what it's like for her! I've written to her, so my letter should be the first one she gets at University.' Of things at home: 'You didn't tell me what colour Philip had painted the gate' and 'I'm looking forward to seeing the new kitchen. How terrible the everlasting dust must be!' But she could cope with her two lives now, and adjust to the demands of each: 'I felt better after about five minutes after leaving Leeds on Monday. What a horrible parting!' And: 'Only eleven days left then I'll be home! Aren't you looking forward to seeing the black devil again! My! the term has gone quickly!'

'Looking forward to seeing you – please don't forget all those things I have asked you to bring, including a perfect non-breakdown car, a dog called Lisa, a young man called Philip, a mummy and a daddy – and don't forget to bring the map so that you know where you're going!'

Requests were many and frequent, for items of clothing left behind, for extra pocket money for activities, but above all for stamps, stamps, stamps. She wrote to many of her friends and relatives, and she wrote home at least once a week: 'Letters bring me nearer to home, if you know what I mean, that's why I love letters.'

Into her own, she poured all the details of her school life. At the beginning of each school year there would be a full record of her new timetable, who would be taking each subject, and what she thought of them, diagrams of the seating in the classroom and the beds in the dormitory. It was all there, and it meant that we could picture her every minute of the day.

'In Maths we're revising logarithms. In Physics, I think, I can't really remember, we're doing lights. For Chemistry we're doing formulas. I think I will like English better this year. We're doing the Pardoner's Tale.'

'The washing machine has broken down. Every night we have to wash our socks and pants, and yesterday we passed buckets of water from hand to hand because the lily pond was so shallow and the fish were certain to die.'

'I'm bowler in rounders. I got some people out (but not as many as I should have done, because I dropped the ball sometimes). I've got a slightly bruised right eye where a hard fast ball was bowled at me, and a little sore left eye from the sun.'

'For my job on Saturday I swept the shoe-cleaning room in the cellar. It was truly very dirty and dusty.'

'Hoorah, because at long last I'm not in the front row for Assembly.'

Her small size obviously still troubled her, as did her continued lack of success in things physical. She kept on trying: 'I practised a lot at the Gym Club and at last I passed my first thing – through vault – quite difficult.' 'Yesterday morning I tried to qualify in the Long Jump. I hoped I'd be able to do it but of course I didn't.' 'I've put my name down for the Gold ASA Swimming Award. I'm sure I'll fail, but it will be something to try for.'

She greatly appreciated the range of activities that were open to the pupils as they grew older: 'The Square Dance Club starts tomorrow at long last.' 'We had our Drama Club. Miss G said my *feet* were acting very well!' 'Yesterday afternoon we had the first Activity Club. We had good fun, played games, talked about necessities for camping – we'll probably go camping in February. We're allowed to wear trousers!'

But later, disappointment struck: 'I'm not going to the Activity Club any more, because there were too many people. Bother! I wish I was still in it.'

Boredom at weekends was still a problem. Church parade offered nothing: 'Boring as usual. I prefer church at home. Has there been a Harvest Festival yet? If not I'd like to go to it.' There is little point in a service one cannot understand or lip-read, and the same applied to films and the theatre.

'We went to *Pygmalion*. I paid 60p and unfortunately was seated right at the back of the Upper Circle. We had a good view of the stage, but couldn't see the faces very well. I should have paid more, but still I enjoyed watching them move about.'

'The film yesterday was *Julius Caesar*. I only watched the first part of it – most of it was in darkness so we could not understand a thing!'

'After tea I went to the folk concert. It was done by a man, but it was rather boring, as I was seated at the back and could only hear bits.'

But she seldom commented on her deafness. As the other pupils were deaf too, she was only conscious of it at points where the hearing world intruded. Sometimes her letters would contain evidence of deafisms – not so much in their structure, for her written language was exceedingly good, but in the obvious mis-lip readings. She talked of 'bigging' her spots ('picking', the lip-read pattern is the same), of Father Christmas arriving in a Chinese 'ruckchair' ('rickshaw'). She asked often for information: 'What are "annuals"? What does "allocated" mean? What does "creosoting" Granny's garage mean? What is a bureau? catering?' And there was the odd, so nearly correct, but slightly misremembered phrase, such as: 'I wouldn't like to be in her feet.'

She accepted her deafness as fact, inconvenient, but seldom more than that: 'I had my hearing test – I think I'm a bit deafer – when I glanced at my audiogram the lines on it were a bit lower I think. Do you know what? I just can't tell the difference between "ee" and "oo".'

'With my gift token I bought "Dance with the Devil" which has no words in it, only drumming. It was on "Top of the Pops" until last week. I hope you'll like it. I like it anyway, and it's quite easy for a deaf child like me to follow.'

At this time she was friendly with a girl who was only partially hearing and therefore had a great interest in pop music. Judith tried desperately hard to keep up: 'We watched "Top of the Pops" and Donny Osmond was on it! V and A and most Donny fans cried for happiness and longing! Donny's brother is getting married tomorrow, have you heard?'

Friends were all important, especially at the weekends when one must have a partner for the Sunday afternoon walk. Mid-teens are a time for passionate friendships, all-absorbing in a boarding school: 'I had a bad night last night. I couldn't get to sleep because I was hot and excited and 'cos V was with me, and V had a wasp sting on her leg and I had to go and find the housemistress and comfort V too. . . .'

'In the table tennis tournament I'll be playing against V. Oh no! If I beat her I'll hate doing it.'

'On Thursday I was very upset because V was going around with a fourth former and didn't speak to me much. I cried during the History lesson, and Miss J thought I'd got a cold. . . . we're not best friends any more. Anyway I feel a bit better now, though I've no one to go around with.'

But perhaps even more important than the individual friend-ships, was the sense of belonging to a gang and of sharing in its activities – sometimes nefarious: 'We had a Midnight Feast. We all went down to the cellar to our usual place. We had a large chocolate biscuit each, then three plain square biscuits. I ate a lemon cream then D passed round some more. It was about 3.30 a.m. when we went up. We cleaned our teeth. We had at least ten small biscuits and two large biscuits each. Quite a lot really isn't it!. . . . Mum said we wouldn't be able to concentrate on our work – well it was Sunday next day, and we get up one hour later on Sundays!'

Punishments for misdemeanours were in the main accepted cheerfully: 'I've already had to write a punishment essay for swinging on my chair.' 'I have to do prep in the Hall for three weeks because I was making a noise in the classroom.' But anything felt to be injustice was very hard to bear.

'On Saturday for a little joke we dropped G's tie and belt from my dormitory window, down to a wire half way between the window and the ground so that it looked like "washing on the line". We were going to get it by reaching up from the ground, but I had to do my job, and then it was really pouring with rain, so in the end it was Sunday morning and we were caught by a matron. She blew up with us and said for the rest of term (six weeks) there is to be no discos, no films, no late TV, no shopping, no evening clothes! All our privileges! Now I'll have to rush around for Christmas presents at the last minute at home. . . . Anyway, do you think that our punishment is fair? G didn't know anything about it and anyway we were going to give them back to her. I wouldn't have minded if we had to lose a few privileges, but to lose *all* of them for a long time is a bit much.'

The hurt was obvious, and for once I interfered, discovering in the process that the 'washing line' had been an overhead electric cable and the prank had been considered a dangerous one. All the same, the punishment rankled, and was considered by Judith to be unjust, since 'some girls had a midnight feast in the gym – a far naughtier thing than we did – and guess what they got: *only* no weekend clothes, that's all!'

On the other hand she was quick to appreciate kindness, particularly when unexpected: 'I was wrapping up K's present (sweets) in a paper bag, but it was Lights Out, so I took it to the loo and finished it there, and I was taking it back to the dormitory (hiding it under my dressing gown) when the sweets fell out and Matron saw me. She took me to the Linen Room. I explained it was for K and she put the sweets in a Black Magic box and stuck the lid on with a bit of Elastoplast (instead of Sellotape). Wasn't it kind of her!'

If her thoughts and opinions were sometimes naive, we nevertheless treasured the honesty which they revealed and the continuing ease of her relationship with us: 'Hi! for the first time in 1975! Thank you ever so much for the lovely time I had during the holiday, which was one of the best I've ever had. . . . If I don't have any pancakes for lunch this term please could Mum make one or two, specially for me, in the Easter holidays?'

'One of my silly parents forgot to sign his or her name on the travelling card. Who was it? I think Mr P would prefer it if he gets a definite card about my travelling home. Or don't you want me?'

She had an impish sense of humour, and often laughed at herself: 'We were watching a TV programme about skin protection and suddenly – I fainted. I leant on G who was standing behind me, and G not realising I was almost asleep, moved away, and they were all horrified to hear a nasty Thud! on the floor!'

'We went on the sponsored walk. It was miserable weather and there was slippery mud all the way! I fell dozens of times and my socks, shoes, trousers and raincoat were ABSOLUTELY FILTHY! It was a good laugh though!'

Not many things got her down. She did her school work conscientiously, and in June 1975, aged $14\frac{3}{4}$, she achieved her first 'O' level – in English.

We felt she thoroughly deserved the exciting holiday that had been arranged for that summer.

Chapter Seventeen

GROWING UP

The inconvenience of the four-term year with its different holiday dates, meant that Judith was often at home while her peers were still at school. Relations and friends were a great help, and so were the visits she paid to local schools, but as she grew older, so she needed to spend the holidays in relaxation, and we tried very hard to find different experiences for her. In her October breaks we made a point of taking her away. In 1973 she joined us on a mini-weekend in Morocco. The narrow alleys of the Kasbah, bargaining with the Moroccan shopkeepers, watching the snake-charmers, were all new experiences, and fascinating ones.

In 1974 we visited Dorset, Somerset and Devon, and she enjoyed being part of a Holiday Fellowship Group. She learned how to mix socially at the breakfast table and chat to different people, and if she missed out on the instructions for the day, at least she could join in the walks, evening games and country dancing, on equal terms.

In 1975, the school had planned a trip to Annecy. We were delighted about this, because it was to take place at the end of June when, normally, she would have been left on her own at home. From Thonon-les-Bains she wrote her usual long epistle, mainly full of comments upon the food, the weather – which unfortunately was poor – and the sight-seeing they did manage to achieve in spite of torrential rain and fog.

Judith also had a French pen-friend, Edith, who had once been to stay with us, and it had been arranged that after Judith's holiday with the school, Edith's family would collect her and take her back with them to their farm at Chaumont. We knew that this would not be easy for Judith. Her written French was good, but her spoken

French exceedingly poor. (Although I had been amazed, when giving her French oral lessons at home, at how much she *could* imitate correctly when using the ATU and a phonetic alphabet.)

She wrote of her experiences: 'At 11.50 a.m. a man and a young girl were standing outside our centre [at Thonon-les-Bains]. I gingerly asked the man, "Are you . . . M. Meyer?" at which he suddenly smiled and a flow of French came out. Of course I couldn't understand him, so I asked them to come in and see Mr K while I got my things. Anyway, we were off by noon, and Martine, the girl, started a conversation with me – on paper! We wrote all sorts of things, mostly in French. At the farm Edith spoke mostly English to me, Martine wrote French to me, and M. Meyer usually says "Ça va?" and my response is "Oui!" That's about all I've spoken to him. . . . I've got three weeks to buck up! The farm is half dairy and half wheat. I help to get the cows in for milking, and have twice seen the young cows – gensies – which are sweet. Now I'm longing for a long, long piece of news from home if you don't mind!'

And later: 'The farm has thirty cows or more. It grows oats and barley and its own vegetables. While fetching the cows in, Martine and I came across a newly-born calf. It's sweet and black and white. I named it "Eddie", for they said I could provide a name for it as long as it began with "E". Some time later I tried to milk a cow with the help of Madame and I could do it! I didn't realise the teat would be so warm! I'd like to do it again, it's a lovely feeling.

'I'm happy at Edith's, and seem to get on well with the rest of the family. Edith tries to speak to me in French but if it's complicated she has to speak in English! I've had two written conversations with Mme. I've seen Marc three times. He took us to Joan of Arc's house at Domrémy and to see a very large vase at Châtillon. We also visited Roman buildings – a very large mosaic and an amphitheatre. I'm sure Philip would have been interested! I've played Monopoly twice or three times; it's of Paris, not of London, and so is rather different yet similar. I've played badminton quite a bit and also a game like our "Ludo" but better. I'll have to show you. It's called "Petits Chevaux". I've helped a bit on the farm – "chercher l'herbe" for the cows, and twice I've helped to fork it up on the trailer which needs a bit of getting used to.'

At the end of July, when she had been in France for five weeks, we collected her from Chaumont, and the three of us explored the Vosges together. I had worried quite a lot while she was on her own in the midst of a strange family, but even if she didn't speak much French she coped admirably, and enjoyed the new surroundings. On the way back to England we had a few days in Paris, and she was fascinated by the huge carp at Fontainebleau, the thousands of people touring Versailles, the multiplicity of Rodin's statues, the eeriness of the catacombs, and above all by the atmosphere of Montmartre, where she enjoyed having her portrait drawn.

The October holidays of 1975 passed in the usual way. The odd visit to her two 'home' schools, the odd piano lesson, for she still derived enjoyment from this: 'I played the piano three times this weekend. I'm glad that I can still play', and the usual exchanges with all her friends and family.

At the end of November she had an extra journey home, for her Confirmation. She had decided that she wished to be confirmed at home, and had been a number of times to talk to the vicar on her own. It was to be only a 36-hour visit, however, for she had her 'O' level General Science the next day. Fog meant delayed trains and an overnight stop at an uncle's, and the next day's journey was difficult too: 'On arriving at the station there seemed to be no taxis outside, nor were there any buses for a long time to come, so I decided I'd walk, as I didn't know where the taxi station was. It was absolutely pouring cats and dogs the two–three miles to school, and nobody offered me a lift, so I was drenched through.'

However, the 'O' level was taken and passed, Grade B, which was fortunate, as a new concern was now looming on the horizon – careers. A month before her 15th birthday she had written: 'I'm undecided what to do when I leave school. I went to the Careers Officer on Thursday afternoon. She was very nice and friendly and found out a lot about myself. I told her that you, Mum, could see me as a research librarian, and she agreed, as well as suggesting that I could be a librarian in a University or something in the laboratory to do with the study of the heart and brain (I can't remember the word, just that I think it begins with ca . . .). Anyway she said I've got the most time than anyone else in my year.'

At the Open Day in 1976 we were told that Judith could achieve 'A' levels, and so there were no immediate decisions to make on her future, but throughout the next year the school provided visits to the places in which she had expressed an interest: 'I've put my name down for an outing to a bank in London to see all the different things you can do in a bank. . . . Two girls talked to us about banking, and even though I couldn't really understand the first girl, the second was much easier to lip-read.'

'It has been arranged for me to go to Reading Hospital and spend the whole day round the Physiotherapy and Radiography Department. As I won't be leaving for two years how nice everyone is to arrange lots for me!'

But the visit was a little unfortunate. . . . 'At the end of the morning the Head of Department and I came to an agreement that Physiotherapy was *not* for me because I can't talk to patients very easily. In the afternoon I got mixed up with Radiography and Physiotherapy and I said – guess what – Radiotherapy! How stupid can one get! The lady said that I was in the wrong part of the hospital for Radiotherapy, and telephoned the other part asking for a Mrs W. There was no one of that name there, so I gave up and read *Jane Eyre* all afternoon instead. However, at 4 p.m. they realised my mistake and made another appointment. I was ready to go through the floor with embarrassment! Now you can laugh at my stupidness!'

Her lack of confidence and returning shyness at this age, 15–16, was very evident: 'Having my name read out in front of everyone in Assembly made me go a right beetroot so I couldn't lip-read very well, my face being so hot!' 'I've got to read the lesson in front of a hundred and fifty pupils. Help! I haven't read the lesson since I was in the first form. . . . I've just finished reading the lesson. Oh! I was nervous and stumbled over two words and rushed it too. I hated it.'

She was very, very conscious of the fact that she was younger than the other girls in her class. They were interested in boys and she wasn't – or only from the sidelines: 'Did you get a Valentine card? I didn't of course, and this time didn't bother to send any! But in the evening there was a Valentine disco and I for once decided to go – and it was more interesting! I watched the second Lumpy Custard show and the "Love Bugs" – five fourth form girl dancers who were good even though three of them are very deaf.'

Quite often however she gave the disco a miss and retired into her books or the TV: 'I'm reading *The Hobbit* now which I can't put down unless I have to'; 'I started and read most of *Forever Free*'; 'I saw *Frankenstein* last night – it was frightening but I enjoyed it – such a bad night after!'; '*Hamlet* is a good story but the film was disappointing as it concerned far too much talking by one person to himself'; '*Macbeth* was an AA film but some of us thought it should have been an X, there being so much blood! Some of the long speeches had been cut down and there was a great deal more action than in the book'; 'Some of us watched a horrible film from *Beasts* – just the kind I like watching, but which I'm sure Mum wouldn't be too keen on as it was so horrible.'

This interest in the macabre gave her a peculiar sense of humour sometimes: 'Excuse writing but I'm writing with my left hand as I have unfortunately broken my right arm. Full details later. It's bad luck isn't it seeing that exams are coming on soon. . . . [one page later] I've had enough of writing with my left arm. I wonder if I had any effect on you? I was just practising in case it did come true.' It did indeed have an effect, and for the next real shock, the ground was very thoroughly prepared.

'And now for something totally unexpected. I won't be surprised if you get an awful shock and I wasn't going to tell you until I came home but I didn't want you to know from another source – I think you'd better finish eating first and at least not do anything else apart from reading this:– During the French paper I was in the middle of my translation, when looking to my side I saw S just day-dreaming. Without thinking I told him to "Come on" and he said to me "What about you? Shut up." These seven short words led us into very serious trouble as we were *not* to communicate and the penalty would be disqualification from the whole of this summer's period of 'O' levels. How awful! We weren't thinking of cheating but we knew how thoughtless and stupid we'd been. Fortunately Mr P believed us so we were *not* disqualified. Now you know what a naughty girl I am, and I'm extremely lucky to have got off so lightly. Well, that's over!'

The shock had been a salutary one and, if nothing else, concentrated her attention wonderfully on the rest of her examinations. That summer she achieved another six 'O' levels, English Literature with a Grade A, Grade B for Geography, Maths, French and Biology and Grade C for Physics but she failed in Chemistry, Needlework and History.

In the meantime the search for a suitable career continued. I had written to the National Lending Library at Boston Spa asking if we might have a look round, and we paid a useful visit there that Easter. Judith thought she might be interested, and was in fact to have work experience there the following year.

She was experiencing considerable difficulty at this time with her hearing aid. At the end of 1975 she wrote: 'I'll be getting a new hearing aid. I hope it'll be much better than my silly black Medresco', and later: 'My new aid is an ear-level [an aid which fits behind the ear] for a trial but I don't know if it does really help me' and 'My aid does whistle. I can't always hear it myself and I used to, but I hope it won't annoy you and you'll tell me whenever it whistles.'

Because she was so deaf she needed to turn the volume up high, and again and again she referred to the problem of an ill-fitting mould: 'I've got another new ear mould but since it whistled if it was comfortable and if it didn't whistle it was uncomfortable I've switched back to my first ear mould again. I'm getting rather fed up . . . shopping in Newbury on Friday I wondered why shop assistants were looking at me oddly. I realised it was my whistling hearing aid and so had it off for the rest of the time, which I don't really like.'

For 15 years she had put up with the inconvenience of always having to wear an aid and never complained, but now her distress was obvious. I was, that Easter, on a course at Manchester University, and took the opportunity to have her hearing tested there. It emerged that the aid she had on trial was not nearly strong enough. Two Oticons were suggested and five months later Judith duly received the first of these: 'I've now got the Oticon ear-level aid at last! It's certainly louder and clearer. I like it but I haven't been out of school with it yet; it makes a lot of difference if I'm out of school or in, I think.'

Certainly we noticed a big difference in Judith's response when she came home. She turned quickly at the sound of a human voice, provided that this was within a range of three to four feet, and was then ready for lip-reading whatever was said to her. In the summer of 1976 too, we had a chance to borrow a Radio Link Aid and were amazed at the response to this. From the bottom of the garden she could hear our voice in the aid, not what we said, but at least that we were speaking to her. And, using the old nursery rhyme technique, she could give the second line of the verse by deciphering the first from the rhythm she heard. We realised that the Radio Link plus lip-reading would be very valuable, and indeed this was to prove the case in the future.

Chapter Eighteen

WHAT SHALL I BE?

Judith's last two years at school were naturally taken up very largely with 'A' levels and with worrying about a job for the future. The first hurdle was *which* 'A' levels she was in fact to take. At first it was to be French, physics and maths. She had done extraordinarily well in French, she seemed to have a natural flair for language, and, selfishly perhaps, I encouraged her in choosing French, as it was the only one of the three in which I could continue to help her. However, the term was not very far advanced when she began to get into difficulties.

'About my A levels. I realise now that I'm sort of dreading the French into English part, as I can't put very good English phrases in place of French phrases. . . . I want to know how you feel about it.' And later, 'I know it would have been a nice relaxing contrast, but I didn't really want to take French in A level, as I wasn't enjoying the French literature very much.' She was quite definite about what she could and couldn't do: 'In Chemistry I can't tell if I've made a terrible mistake in my equations. . . . anyway I'm *not* doing Chemistry again and that's that.'

She decided to drop French, and add geography to the maths and physics, and throughout the next two years was to enjoy the field-work which this entailed very much. Perhaps it saved her sanity!

'Oh both Maths and Physics are driving me bonkers! It's something to do with probability in Maths and I absolutely loathe it. And Physics is not very easy to understand either at the moment.'

She was horrified by the amount of work which 'A' levels entailed: 'Our form teacher told us that at least seven to ten hours

Sixteen!

of work is needed for each A level subject, so I need to do two to three hours a day and more at weekends. Gosh – I didn't realise it was that much!' She was very conscientious and worked desperately hard: 'Exams have been really horrible . . . the preying of exams constantly on my mind . . . I had a dream the other night. I got B for Maths and F for both Physics and Geography; I hope it won't be true. . . . I'm looking forward to coming home – though I must get down to some work.'

Home was still close to her thoughts: 'Shame, I'll be here when you move house, I'd have liked to know what moving house is like. Please don't bother to sort all my stuff out; you can always dump my rubbish on the bed. Do tell me as much as you can about the upheaval. . . . I'd be extremely grateful to Philip if he could decorate my room.'

She remained throughout closely in touch with what everyone was doing: 'Glad Frances is making use of her sewing machine. I'm looking forward to seeing her skirt and blouse. Why does Lisa chew the letters up I wonder? Any other naughty habits she may have started? Please do bring Philip's letters with you.'

But in spite of the closeness to home, she adored the activities and friendships which school provided. She had developed physically and now enjoyed team games: in volleyball she discovered she could serve and hit the ball on her fist, she had had a good spell of playing hockey in the under-sixteen team, and now it was the turn of badminton and tennis.

She also enjoyed walking: 'This Saturday we've decided to catch two buses to Kingsclere and walk all the way back to school via Watership Down. I know it's probably only just a hill but it will be nice to see what it's like and if there's any resemblance to the book, which I really enjoyed.'

These last two years she had less and less time for reading – although Frances and Philip urged her to read more and broaden her outlook – but at this stage she was enjoying more modern novels such as *Airport* and *Hotel* and *Rich Man Poor Man*. If she saw something on TV she always wanted to read it, as she knew just how much she missed of the story from watching alone.

Lack of hearing what other people are talking about always leads to naivety and she was becoming aware of just how little she knew of the world outside school: 'We were discussing the price of keeping house . . . we had to do a sort of test to show how much we knew about politics and things. I'm afraid I don't know very much. . . . Mr P was telling us about ages of buildings etc. v. interesting.'

Of her future career she was definite on one thing. 'A' levels were to be the limit. She did not want to go to university and she was writing off at this time for information on radiography and optics. In the summer of 1977 she had a month's work experience at the British Lending Library. She coped well with this; she lived in 'digs' from Monday to Friday and enjoyed the experience, but she found the actual work she was given to do 'boring'. It was mainly filing, and she was not enchanted by it, but undoubtedly this work experience gave her a new maturity.

This was further developed by a holiday taken on her own with a particular friend. She had been camping with the school the previous summer and it had been 'great'. Sleeping in tents was 'squashed, but good fun' and canoeing had been a novel and exciting experience. Now she wanted to try camping with a friend – 'just us two'. They had looked on the library map and found quite a few prospective places in the Peak District. This was going to be miles away from anywhere, and so we stipulated that the camping idea was fine, but it must be on a regulation camp site. Eventually they decided on Robin Hood's Bay, and I left them there one day in August. Fortunately D was an experienced camper, for Judith didn't really have a clue about cooking or safety precautions. She was totally undaunted by what 'might happen' and never one to envisage the worst.

Her unbounded optimism undoubtedly stood her in good stead, but often meant that she was very 'accident prone'. 'At G's house unfortunately I accidently pulled the towel rail off the wall. Also before getting on the train the small suitcase I was borrowing fell open. All my things came pouring out but fortunately there weren't all that many people about! I also cut my thumb with the bread knife and lost my Libra ring in the train never to be found again. Clumsy little me! I'm a very unlucky girl aren't I? Never mind, I did enjoy the weekend very much.'

These visits to friends' houses and escapes from school at weekends were most eagerly looked forward to: 'I had a nice time on Friday evening – my first sort of date too. We met up at the cinema and then we looked for a cheap café for something to eat (we're not bulging with money you know!). And then we all walked all the way back to school. We all thoroughly enjoyed ourselves, and we hope to do it again sometime. It was the first time we'd gone out without any staff supervising us, and that's a fact even though I've been here nearly six years. Don't worry, we were sensible!'

A growing sense of independence was becoming evident, leading to an increase in self-confidence: 'Could Frances send me another of those railway timetables from London–Bradford?. . . . In case you're all out would you leave the key in the usual place. . . . Instead of coming home on Sunday I could stay till Thursday, assuming that's all right by you?'

She was still undecided about what she wanted to do in the future: 'We had a day out at Reading University on Thursday. It was nice to be out of school for a change and to see what University life was supposed to be like, but it didn't exactly appeal to me so, even now, I don't know yet whether or not I'll go.'

A talk with the Head, however, and the discussion of a 'sandwich' course rather than a pure physics one, helped her to come to a decision, and in due course she applied to the universities of Bradford, Durham and Leeds. In the meantime she benefited from practice with mock interviews and from visits to scientific establishments – not always successful, as twelve in a group was 'too many, we couldn't get to understand everything'.

During the Christmas holidays of her last year at school I took her for an interview with the radiography department at the Infirmary. Judith had been very keen on doing this but neither of us had appreciated the practical difficulties: that the wearing of masks would preclude lip-reading, and that she would be unable to hear if patients in cubicles called out for help. A visit to my brother's research centre in the south had implanted a desire to work in medical physics but she began to accept that the only way to achieve this would be through a physics degree.

In her last year at school she had interviews at both Bradford and Leeds. I accompanied her to the first Bradford one and it was not easy. Most of the interviewers were helpful, but one seemed to set out to create as many difficulties as possible; never looking at her when he spoke, and questioning her ability to travel to different places for her sandwich year. I knew Judith's limitations but lack of initiative and determination were not two of them! For the second interview at Bradford and for the Leeds interview, she coped on her own which she much preferred to do. She reported that at Leeds they had never had a deaf student before, and she was able to inform them that since her hearing aid was insufficient to get much help from anyway, lecturers' hand-outs would be far more helpful than microphones – they didn't have to worry!

By the spring of her last year at school, she had provisional offers from both Leeds and Bradford and was then able to settle down and concentrate on both getting her 'A' levels and passing her driving test. For her first driving lesson she was 'a bit nervous, but I don't think I did awfully badly . . . it was the foot pedals that gave the worst trouble – so much to remember isn't there! The gear and clutch sometimes made awful noises and I was a bit confused on the instructions, but I'll get used to his waving hands in time!'

The instructor to whom she went, although used to the deaf pupils from Mary Hare, put them through exactly the same procedure as hearing candidates. He devised a simple code of gestures to cover important instructions: 'emergency stop' was indicated by a hand thrust firmly forwards on to the dashboard; in 'turn left', 'turn right', the command was accompanied by the appropriate gesture clearly given by hand.

For her fourth lesson she 'did terribly . . . it was probably due to its being dark, and I was not at all used to seeing so little, I hadn't realised things looked quite different in the dark.' However, in a month or two she had mastered even three-point turns, and was eagerly looking forward to practising at home. Frances and Philip had also used my car to practise on at home, but I confess to being much more nervous when the time came to allow Judith the same opportunities. However, she turned out to be a good, safe driver on the straight main roads, judging distances accurately and approaching the task sensibly and with great concentration. It was only on the twisting moorland roads that my hair turned appreciably greyer – the possibility of a stray sheep, a rearing horse, a child on a cycle lurking just around the corner simply never entered her head; imagined danger was too unreal to worry about, and by the end of an hour's practice I was only too ready to collapse thankfully into a chair! It was impossible, of course, to talk to her while she was driving. Instructions had to be given very clearly beforehand, and an emergency procedure agreed upon.

Later, she was to copy a friend's example and affix a mirror to the centre of the dashboard so that some communication at any rate was a possibility. But that was, as yet, in the future.

For her test, she wrote, 'My knees really did shake literally.' There was no problem in understanding the examiner however: 'He gestured to me whatever his instructions were, and was careful to face me all the time he spoke', and she was really delighted to pass first time. Having a car meant that communication with friends was a great deal easier. The telephone had always been out of the question, but now she could look up her friends and relations at home. Later, for her 21st birthday, I gave her my little Mini, and we were pleased that no special terms were required for her insurance. With the possession of a driving licence and with the three 'A' levels she achieved in 1978, the future indeed looked rosy.

Chapter Nineteen

THE UNDERGRADUATE

And what of her undergraduate days? How did she cope among her own contemporaries in a completely strange environment?

We had decided, and she agreed totally, that there was little point in attending a university, if one did not 'live in'. To commute daily, even though it was possible, would not have given her the sense of belonging, and therefore we urged the Local Authority to provide her with an additional grant for residence. This they eventually agreed to do, and the day before her 18th birthday Judith moved into Hall at Bradford University. She had a pleasant room, the girls in the surrounding rooms seemed helpful, and we left her to stand on her own feet. She herself seemed overcome as we left, but the following night she rang and gave a message that she was all right, and I felt easier about her. We used this contact by phone on a number of occasions. She could not, of course, hear our voices, nor even if she had obtained the right number, but at least she could deliver messages. We evolved a 'hooting' system because hoots she could hear; after each statement she made she would pause and I would 'hoot' the response: one hoot for 'Yes, I understand'; three for 'No' and a series of hoots for 'I don't understand; say it again.' I found the system comforting because it told me she was all right (this was the time of the 'Yorkshire Ripper' in Bradford), but it did very little for her psychologically; she found it embarrassing when using the university call-box, and after a year she used it no more but asked a friend to ring up with a message.

For several months I was to visit her once a week. This provided both of us with an opportunity for catching up on news and of answering queries, and it also meant that I was able to see that she was coping with the demands made upon her. Her weekends we did not intrude upon; it was essential that she should mix with the others as much as possible, and although she found this difficult at first, she persevered. Loneliness was often there. She would take a book down to meals when she felt unable to break into a group. It was difficult for her to follow a group conversation; words moved too quickly back and forth, and lip-reading was an impossibility. As yet she lacked the courage to initiate a conversation on her own, and there was nobody, at this stage, who would see that she was not left out in the cold.

Sometimes my heart ached for her, but she didn't give up, and she never fled home at weekends. It was her university and she wanted to belong, and so she kept on trying. Fortunately we could draw parallels with Frances's and Philip's own experiences. She remembered that they had been lonely too at first, and she accepted that many of her problems were due to newness and not necessarily to deafness. When she saw groups of girls talking together in corridors, she was not unique in wishing to be one of them. They were not deliberately excluding her because she was deaf; they just had never even thought about it. If she wanted to belong, then she must seek them out, knock on their doors, find out their interests, and perhaps, if she explained the problems she had, they would come in time to appreciate them. And so they did. She was worried about not knowing if there was a fire alarm; one of the girls arranged to be responsible for this. She worried about not waking up for lectures if her alarm (a vibrating metal box placed under the mattress, which shook the bed) went on the blink; they took it in turns to come in and wake her up in the morning. And gradually, very gradually, contacts were made.

On the whole she got on better with the overseas students, because 'they speak more slowly and they have a lot more patience'. Among the English students she found the social science ones the easiest to get along with, because they tended to be 'extrovert and sociable', and they had a greater facility with words; they could change the sentences around if she hadn't got the meaning the first time. And then, too, the conversation of the physicists was mainly about physics; the social scientists talked about a variety of things. There were difficulties, even so. If she went out with a group of friends then it was impossible to carry on a conversation walking back afterwards in the dark; with a single companion it was much easier. And sometimes strangers exaggerated their mouth movements, making things worse, not better, or spoke in monosyllables so that it was difficult to maintain a conversation.

By the spring she was much more settled. She had acquired a boyfriend now, an Indian, and brought him over to tea. Just to possess a boyfriend somehow seemed to make all the difference, for it proved she was just like the others, and she wrote proudly of cooking omelettes for him, teaching him backgammon and learning pool.

By now, she was going to ballroom dancing, and Fred, from Hong Kong, came on the scene. They were to be friends for a considerable time but she announced firmly: 'I don't want to get tied down or serious with anyone.' And what of her work? Of her lecturers she reported that they were 'helpful and friendly'. They didn't all realise how dependent she was on written information – one of them hardly ever wrote anything on the blackboard and she had to copy up notes hastily from other people. The university had generously provided her with a Phonic Ear, and most lecturers were very good at slinging the microphone for this round their necks when they arrived to lecture; little did they realise that if they inadvertently took it with them when they left the room – literally – she was able to follow their progress to the lavatory and the ensuing flush of the toilet!

She was still totally dependent on lip-reading, and those who moved around when talking, or who spoke with their eyes shut, were not easy to follow. Laboratory work was a terrible problem, as fellow students mumbled. Tutorials were worse: 'I'm too scared to say anything,' she wrote. But in the main she worked hard in her first year and was delighted to achieve good results, and to be transferred on to the Honours Course.

The second year was a different matter. By now she had three firm friends and had been asked to share a house with them. This was good in itself, but the resulting distractions meant that her work suffered greatly. She went all out to try and mix socially, she joined numerous societies, went on hikes at weekends, coped with a house where sometimes there were mice and slugs, helped mop up after boyfriends who were sick, tried to keep up with their discussions on politics, sex and religion and it was all too much. She was stuck on maths, she didn't understand nuclear physics, lectures were boring, boring, boring, and it was really no surprise when she failed her second year.

She felt badly about it and tried hard over the summer of 1980 to catch up on the reading, but her sandwich year started almost immediately. For this she was placed in a hospital, her dearest wish. She had hoped to get work experience in physics but this was not to be, and she was placed in computing. There was little work and she was often bored. Tea-breaks were 'nerve-wracking'; she talked to no one and they didn't talk to her. In September she retook her second-year exams and managed to pass this time, for which she was very thankful. She struggled through her six months work experience, often bored and even more often very lonely, but perhaps she misjudged her colleagues, for when she left she was unbelievably touched when they gave her a signed card and a handsome book token.

'Sometimes it's hard to follow you' – with her brother and cousin

For the second six months of her sandwich year she was placed at Warrington. She was given a room in a hostel and again we left her in yet another strange environment: new contacts to make, new faces to lip-read, the old familiar shyness to overcome. Again the first month was almost too much: 'I sat on my own for tea. . . . I read a newspaper at lunch'. . . . 'I'm not getting any closer to making any friends; I'm stuck with the same group who sometimes bring me in but more often don't – I can't really join in their jokes or anything. . . . I didn't really feel comfortable since they mumbled all the time.' And she could not even lose herself in the work. 'I get the impression there's a fair bit of computing to do – Oh No, No, No! – it looks as if it's going to be difficult to do physics.'

But this time she was going to try harder: 'I've sort-of made friends with the door-woman at the Club. I probably look really sad and lost and helpless! Tonight she found the Bridge Secretary for me . . . if I don't like the bridge then I could try dancing.' But at bridge everyone was 'most friendly and helpful' (they were older and more understanding – I pointed out to Judith that she was expecting too much from youngsters of 19 and 20; they were still finding their own feet and they weren't mature enough to appreciate her additional problems).

Gradually, however, she became accepted by a particular group of young people. Their weekly excursions into pubs were not much good for her – pubs are generally dark, and lip-reading most difficult, but she joined them at discos and at bridge, on visits to Manchester for ten-pin bowling, and on hostelling in the Lakes. She was a good sport and even the prospect of being blindfolded and fed with yoghurt by a similarly blindfolded partner was good for a laugh. She made herself acceptable and she was accepted, and above all, now Jeremy came on the scene – someone who would keep her in touch with what other people had said, who would tell her what the jokes were about, and who was sensitive enough to ensure that she was never left out in the cold.

The work experience eventually finished and she went back to university but not before she had added yet another first to her list of achievements – a parachute jump: 'Well, I've done it! We went parachuting on Saturday morning! The weather was perfectly dry, sunny and quite windless. I didn't really have time to feel nervous . . . the plane flight was most enjoyable, sort of gliding lop-sided, fantastic views of the nearby sands and sea. But it was really windy when the door of the plane was opened, it did nerve me a little, but I climbed out OK even though I forgot nearly everything else we'd been taught. . . . I couldn't control myself at all; it was because I forgot to look out for those special strings above me, and pulled the actual supports instead, which didn't make any difference really! So I just gave up and concentrated on enjoying the fantastic views. . . .'

New home at Harrogate

The sandwich year had provided Judith with financial independence and she made the most of this by embarking on an inter-railing trip round Europe. Together with a deaf friend from Mary Hare she travelled to Denmark and Sweden, to Norway and Germany, to Austria, Yugoslavia, Italy and the South of France. She linked up with two of the foreign families we knew, and she returned all the richer from her many and varied experiences, having survived the disappearance of her luggage, the impounding of her passport and the importuning of beggars in Rome.

She was 21 now and in the September we spent a memorable day. The morning was given over to relations; to all those people who had helped her so much throughout her life. In the afternoon we had a Car Treasure Hunt for 35 young people, and in the evening we had a party which continued until the small hours. Over 20 youngsters stayed the night, 11 were still there for Sunday lunch; it was an exhausting but infinitely worthwhile weekend, and I was moved to tears by the bouquet which arrived in the midst of it all – 'Thank you, Mum' it said quite simply, 'With love, Judith'.

The following June she achieved a well-deserved degree and we attended her graduation ceremony. We spotted Judith looking surprisingly slight in the enveloping gown – what a change from the habitual jeans and sweater! The long file of graduates moved slowly up the steps and across the stage. The ceremony was imposing, orderly, evocative. Suddenly the Hall erupted into applause as a physically handicapped boy was pushed out from the wings to collect his award. A few moments later, a guide dog led his blind master across the stage. And again the thunderous applause. Judith's golden head approached the platform. There are no outward signs of deafness, and the applause for Judith was as normal as the slight young figure who collected the degree. Only a few of us could appreciate the lifetime's effort that had been necessary to achieve it. When I said to Judith afterwards, 'They didn't realise you too had a handicap, did they?', her reply was typical. 'But what would be the good of them clapping any harder, Mum,' she said, 'I couldn't have heard them anyway, could I?'

What sanity! What good humour! And what a glorious sense of proportion! We felt that the world owed acceptance to this determined young 22-year-old, and to all those who, like her, have a lifetime's struggle before them.

Scotland, 1982

Postscript from the publisher's editor:
The lovely news of Judith's engagement to Jeremy arrived as the proofs were being read. They are to be married in December 1984 and will carry with them the good wishes of us all.

Part Two
UNDERSTANDING THE DEAF

Chapter Twenty

TRANSITION

The story in Part One is an authentic account of the gradual development – social, physical and cerebral – of a profoundly deaf child, written with the aid of the notes, diaries and letters kept at the time. The story begins with an unknown quantity, a baby in a pram, and ends on a note of high success. It is not, however, the intellectual success that I wish to stress, but the development of a rounded personality integrated into the hearing world.

I believe that integration is the birthright of any deaf child, and I believe that it can be achieved by far more children than at present, if the initial circumstances are right.

At the present time the goal of normality – of communicating by speech within a hearing world – has ceased to be a target for many who work in this professional field. There are those who think, not that the deaf should enter the hearing world, but that the hearing world should go out to them by means of sign language. I regard this as asking for the unattainable. There is a sizeable minority of Welsh-speaking people within our community but do we consider it our duty to speak Welsh? And would we be willing to learn Gaelic? There is undoubtedly a case for those who work most closely with minorities to learn their language, but not, I submit, for the world as a whole. Majority opinion will always hold sway, and I consider it our duty to convey this hard and unpalatable fact to the deaf children for whom we care most deeply and with whose development we are concerned.

Having said that, I am convinced that society as a whole owes a great debt to the deaf that is not being fulfilled. They have a right to understanding and respect. Life for a deaf person is exceedingly hard, and the problems which they face are rarely fully appreciated. I believe that this is not through lack of goodwill, but through ignorance tainted with unease in their presence. I hope that the preceding account, and the notes which follow, may help a little towards dispelling that ignorance and increasing that goodwill.

Chapter Twenty-one

UNDERSTANDING THE EAR

To understand why deafness occurs it is first useful to consider the ear – the organ of hearing. The ear may be divided into three parts: external, middle and internal.

THE EXTERNAL (OUTER) EAR

The external ear is what can be seen: its correct name is the *auricle* or *pinna*. It is not essential to hearing, indeed it may be congenitally absent or deformed. This external ear also contains the ear canal (*external acoustic meatus*) and the ear drum (*tympanic membrane*).

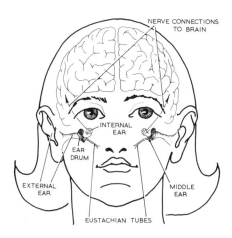

The external ear in relation to the face and head

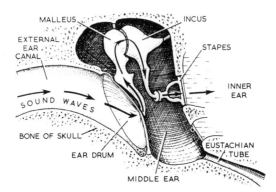

The middle ear showing how the sound waves are conducted

The *ear canal* runs inward towards the ear drum; it may become blocked by wax or by foreign bodies such as marbles, peas, etc, being pushed into it. Such blockages can be removed and are not a cause of deafness, except transiently.

The *ear drum* lies at the end of the ear canal. It is about 6mm in diameter, and it has to vibrate in order to pass on the sounds which it receives via the ear canal.

THE MIDDLE EAR

The correct name for the middle ear is the *tympanic cavity*. It is a tiny area or cavity with a diameter of about 15mm. It contains three tiny, but very important, bones, the *ossicles*. These bones carry the names *malleus*, *incus* and *stapes*, and it is essential that they are able to vibrate and so pass on the sound waves.

The middle ear connects with the back of the throat via the Eustachian tube and it is essential that this tube functions properly so that the air pressure in the middle ear is the same as that outside. (Think of the temporary inconvenience of rapid ascent, or descent, as in a plane.)

What can go wrong?

1. The ossicles may be missing, or may not move freely.
2. The Eustachian tube may become blocked.
3. The cavity may become full of fluid.
4. The cavity may become full of pus. Indeed, the infection may be so severe that the ear drum may perforate.

In all cases *conductive* deafness will occur, because sound cannot be conducted along the ossicles to the inner ear.

TREATMENT

Conductive deafness may be treated by:

1. A decongestant and/or an antibiotic.
2. Draining the pus, and inserting a grommet. This is a relatively simple procedure.
3. Surgery, e.g. removal of the adenoids.

EAR DRUM — GROMMET

A grommet inserted in the ear drum

THE INTERNAL (INNER) EAR

This lies beyond the middle ear and among other parts it contains the *semicircular canals* which are important for balance but not for hearing, and the *cochlea*.

THE COCHLEA

This is shaped like the shell of the common snail being coiled two and a half times. It is a cavity and contains the *organ of Corti*.

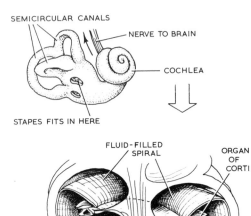

The semicircular canals, the cochlea and the organ of Corti

ORGAN OF CORTI

This is the most sensitive, intricate and highly developed part of the hearing system. It is about 3.75cm (1½in) in length, consists of some 7500 independent units, and contains about 30 000 minute hair cells. The organ of Corti's function is to convert mechanical energy into electrical energy and to despatch the appropriate message to the brain.

Thus it can be understood that damage to the internal ear and hence to the cochlea will cause *sensori-neural* (nerve) deafness. No treatment is possible at present, and the deafness is permanent.

What can go wrong?

Damage to the internal ear can be caused by:

1. Genetic factors.
2. Pre-natally (before birth), e.g. by rubella (German measles), syphilis.

3. Peri-natally (at the time of birth), e.g. by prematurity, anoxia, jaundice.
4. Illness, e.g. measles, mumps, influenza, meningitis.
5. Unknown viruses.

It is important to remember:

1. That in approximately 30 per cent of cases of profound deafness, the cause is unknown.
2. One important cause of deafness is rubella.

Rubella (German measles)

1. It is very difficult to know if one has it, because the rash is not distinctive.
2. If a pregnant mother suffers from rubella during the first three months of pregnancy, the effects on the child can be devastating.
3. It causes not only deafness but blindness, brain damage and other defects.
4. There is no need for any pregnant mother to have rubella; a vaccine has been available since 1970.
5. All school girls should be vaccinated.
6. In the USA even boys are inoculated so that they may not pass on rubella to their mothers.

Chapter Twenty-two

SOCIAL DIFFICULTIES OF THE DEAF

To appreciate what it is like to be deaf is not easy. There are many social difficulties which the deaf experience which perhaps have never even occurred to us. They cannot hear the doorbell, so they do not know that someone is on the doorstep. If they happen to have left the door unlocked, then someone may actually be in the house and they are not aware of it. Their privacy can be invaded very easily, and embarrassing situations can often arise. In the street, they cannot hear approaching traffic, nor footsteps which might follow them in the dark. They may not even be aware of wailing sirens or fire alarms. When they are cooking, they cannot hear if a pan boils over or the kettle is whistling. They need to be constantly alert all the time, everywhere. They will not hear anyone shouting if there is danger from cracking ice, crumbling cliffs, rifle ranges or even horse-play at the swimming baths. They will be unaware of adverse road conditions and dangers from ice, floods or snow which may have been reported over the radio. Day-to-day information, such as increases in postal charges, reminders to 'put the clock back', and so on, may never reach them. They may wait for hours on wrong platforms at railway stations, unaware that trains have been cancelled, platforms changed. Small wonder that they need an outsize sense of humour, an unbounding degree of optimism. The warmth of human contact is often denied them. They are left out at parties, at dances, in the canteen. Workmen may take advantage of them when they come to do jobs within the house; communication is difficult, and misunderstandings may arise. When they seek relaxation in the pub there are new difficulties, created by subdued lighting and constant movement. How can one lip-read when one cannot see the other person's lips or when people are constantly passing backwards and forwards?

Perhaps it is small wonder that the deaf are driven back into the security of their own clubs, where they know they can make themselves understood and where they can truly relax.

Just as the immediate reaction to a blind person may be one of instant sympathy – how glad we are that *we* are not blind, how dreadful it would be to be deprived of that glorious view, the vivid colours of that window display, the vision of that waving field of wheat, so the immediate reaction to a deaf person is often one of irritation. Why *can't* he get what we're talking about? Why *does* she have to make so much noise, clattering cutlery, banging pots? Why does he have to rattle the newspaper so loudly and eat so noisily? Why must deaf people talk so loudly in such unmusical tones? That they cannot *hear* the noise they are making is difficult for us to appreciate. Similarly we do not see why a group of deaf people should find it necessary to spread across the pavement and obstruct our free passage, sometimes even walking backwards into us. *We* are quite able to talk to people from a sideways position. We do not have to face them in order to lip-read and it is difficult to appreciate their particular problems.

Their handicap may be said to violate our sense of space. We can ignore the blind person if we wish; he will not know after all. Deafness obtrudes itself in a different way. And because of this it makes us feel uncomfortable; perhaps we even have a sense of guilt. But perhaps if only we were more aware of the difficulties which they face, then we should more readily appreciate their problems.

HOW CAN THE PUBLIC HELP?

As I have stated, I believe that it is unrealistic to expect the general public to learn to sign in order that they may communicate with that small minority of people who are not able to hear, but there are many things which they *can* do.

The first is to appreciate the depth of the problem. This is not easy. A deaf person looks perfectly normal. The ear-level hearing aid is not in sight, there is nothing to denote that this person is different. Indeed, he does not want to be different. He does not need escorting across the road, he does not have to have special parking facilities. But he *is* different. And when, in all good faith, you address a remark to him you are immediately embarrassed. Why? Because you do not know how to deal with what follows. Perhaps at work you addressed a joking remark, and he simply moved on without giving the expected rejoinder, or he is standing staring at you, not understanding, and expecting you to repeat it, or he has mouthed some (to you) incomprehensible reply. What should you do? The answer, I'm afraid, is try again. If you simply walk away, you are denying help to a section of the community who desperately need it. Forget your own embarrassment and remember only his need, his isolation. Try to imagine he is a foreign visitor who knows little English. You need to face him, to look him in the eye (see Chapter 24). You need to show him that you *want* to communicate – that will take you half-way to the goal. You need to speak clearly, in simple sentences, and to be prepared to change them around if he doesn't get the meaning. You need to show him that you really care, that you want to share ideas, opinions, jokes with him. To do this is very demanding both of time and effort; it is far more demanding than pushing the wheelchair up the ramp, or taking the arm of the blind person. But just as the effort is greater, so also are the rewards. To feel that you have broken through a barrier of isolation and conveyed the warmth of human contact, can be infinitely rewarding, and only those who have got over their own embarrassment and made this contact can appreciate how deeply satisfying it is.

Chapter Twenty-three

HOW TO HELP THE DEAF CHILD

A POSITIVE APPROACH BY THE FAMILY

Remember the following:

1. You are not alone – there is more professional advice available than was ever the case before. Insist on having it.
2. Other parents have felt devastated too – try to get in touch with any who live near you.
3. It is quite normal to feel guilt, anger, grief, resentment, anxiety and despair – and you may go on feeling so for years.
4. Try to turn these very strong emotions into positive fields – it is much better to feel anger and grief than to be simply apathetic. The mere fact that you feel strongly will spur you on to action.
5. Don't go from pillar to post looking for other opinions; you will waste an awful lot of time and will almost certainly be no better off in the end.
6. If you can *accept* your child's deafness as a fact, you are already half way to helping him to success.
7. See him first and foremost as a child. Resolve to treat him as such, and not as 'a special case'. If he is your first child, try to find out about normal child development so that you *know* what is normal behaviour.
8. Enlist the help of all the family. Father, brothers, sisters, grandparents, uncles, aunts, cousins. They can all help if you tell them how. But never, never let them spoil him.
9. Don't think about the future, concentrate on the *now*, there are lots of things you can start doing to help him straight away.

10. Try and relax and *enjoy* your child. He may be handicapped but he will have a real personality. Look for all the good things, and encourage their growth.

11. Don't give up talking. Remind yourself that it's going to be ages and ages before you get any response but you've just got to keep on giving.

12. Try and get on the right side of the hearing aid. See it as an invaluable prop, not as a menace, and get your child to value it too (see Chapter 25).

13. If you try a game or activity and it just doesn't work, then put it away until the time is right and try something else. Learn to adapt. Have the goal in view always, but be prepared to switch tactics. The main object is to understand the other member of the team, your child, so that when you pass him the ball he knows what to do with it.

14. Don't forget there will be plateaus in his development; times of growth followed by what seems to be stagnation. Allow for them, allow for consolidation of what he has learned, and don't give up.

15. Don't be unrealistic and expect him to achieve the impossible. But remember that the opposite attitude is sometimes equally fatal. If you expect too little, that is what you will get. Deaf children are often what we ourselves have made them.

ENCOURAGING NORMALITY

In the preceding account of Judith's life, a great deal of emphasis has been placed on the details of her early environment and on her relationship with her brother and sister. The position of any child within a family is always important, but I am convinced that it is especially so with a deaf child. Nothing I have seen in the 20 years I have been teaching deaf children has caused me to alter that opinion. It is in the home that character is formed and the child's ability to adapt to life is created, and I believe that the deaf child is more dependent than any other on the traits of character he develops. For him, learning must begin almost at birth, and if opportunities are lost in the early years, they are almost always lost for good. For him, learning implies readiness to watch; he will learn little or nothing incidentally, through his ears alone. This is in direct contrast with the hearing child, who is absorbing information all the time from what he hears going on around him. A deaf child lives in a world of his own, and will remain imprisoned within it unless his attention is directed elsewhere.

In the first place then, a deaf child must be brought out of isolation, and into contact – with the family, the neighbours, the local children, the people in the street – and into an ever-widening circle of acquaintances. But in order for him to fit into that world, he must become as normal as possible in terms of behaviour. His lack of speech and language are an inevitable concomitant of deafness and must be accepted as such – it will be a long time before his speech can be understood, and before he has enough words to express himself clearly. But there is no reason whatsoever why he should not be a normal child in every other respect. The fact that he is deaf should not preclude a normal upbringing. His brothers and sisters have the right to as much attention as he has; he should not be allowed to 'lord' it just because he is handicapped. If the child is allowed to be a little prima donna, to show off continually to those around him and never be rebuked 'because he is deaf, poor thing', then he may come to believe that his main function in life is to be the centre of attraction and act accordingly. If he is always allowed to take the lion's share, the biggest piece, the extra sweet, then he will assume that he is the most important member of the family and behave as such. He will acquire an outsize chip on his shoulder that may never be removed. He will assume that the world owes him a living and not that he owes the world a contribution too. And in the end he will suffer himself and feel that society has let him down.

In the upbringing of any child, one treads a tightrope between encouraging self-expression and maintaining order, between over-indulgence and repression. In a permissive age when 'anything goes' it is unfashionable to emphasise the necessity for discipline, but I believe that it is fundamental to the upbringing of a deaf child. The life he will have to face is never going to be easy. He is going to have to learn self-control, self-discipline and self-motivation and it will be much easier for him if he begins to learn them within the routine of a well-ordered home where the rights of others are just as important as his own. Those early years can never be relived, his growth as an adjusted personality is dependent upon them, and it is in this field that the parent has the ultimate responsibility.

ATTITUDES TO ENCOURAGE

Willingness to watch so that he may learn 🌟

All through his life he is going to be dependent on watching –for cues as to meaning given by facial expression and gesture, and for lip-reading. If he can be gently encouraged to watch on every conceivable occasion, then he will acquire the habit early, and he will not waste his early school years.

Acquiring confidence in himself 🌟

It is his parents who will give him self-confidence first of all, by the love which they show him. Only when he feels himself to be accepted and loved for what he is, will he begin to know his own worth. Later on, his self-confidence can be boosted by the knowledge of just how many things he can do – and the ones that he can't will matter less and less. The world will accept him the more readily if he can show that there are some areas in which he can excel – be it swimming or cooking, woodwork or cycling, dress-design or pottery. There are many areas where a deaf person is at no disadvantage, and all these should be explored. The essential thing is to know your own child, to present him with innumerable opportunities, even those which seem unlikely areas, but to seize immediately on those in which he shows an interest, never forcing him into any particular mould.

Caring for other people

There will be a great temptation to make your handicapped child the centre of the universe, but you could do him no greater disservice. Although he must become self-confident, he must not be allowed to become egocentric or aggressive. There are unlimited opportunities for encouraging unselfishness within the confines of the home – sharing with brothers and sisters: sweets, toys, games.

Learning to take turns when playing, learning to be pleased when others win. Taking an interest in other children's friends and hobbies. Sharing jobs that have to be done – putting away toys, laying tables, washing up, making beds. Running errands for older people, drawing cards for relations who are ill, making buns for people in hospital. If he can be encouraged to give, and not just to take, you are helping him in a worthwhile way.

Zest for living

Many handicapped people have lived extremely full lives, but their being able to do so very often depends on their own inner resources. If a deaf child can be encouraged to find joy in everything he does, whether it is banging on a drum, running a mile or looking at the pleasing patterns of a picture he has drawn, if he can come to appreciate beauty in all its forms, he will find that self-pity is non-existent, because it has been crowded out. The world has very little time for those who are obsessed with their own problems, but a great deal of appreciation for those who attempt to lead a full life.

Acquiring independence ✳

It is all too easy to take the initiative away from the handicapped person; to assume that because they are lacking in one area they must be treated differently in others. Deaf children need to be encouraged to make decisions from the earliest possible moment. Which biscuit would you like, the round one or the square one? Which socks would you like to wear tomorrow? What present shall we buy for Grandma? Where shall we go for a picnic? For our holiday? and so on. Because conversation is often so limited in scope, a deaf child's outlook can become very narrow: the ability to make small choices today will develop into the ability to make major decisions tomorrow.

A sense of humour

The ability to laugh at oneself, to find one's own mistakes funny, is essential to a deaf person. The occasions will be many: misheard commands, instructions, requests, advice – being given the wrong drink, getting on the wrong bus, turning up at the wrong time. Sometimes the only way out is to laugh; if one did not one would weep, and laughter is a sure antidote to self-pity.

LOOKING AT BOOKS TOGETHER

The importance of encouraging reading can never be over-stressed. A deaf child receives only imperfect patterns of words from lip-reading (see Chapter 24). Those patterns must be filled out by *seeing* the written word upon the page.

There are times, of course, when this is not practicable. One might be peeling potatoes at the sink: if one dries one's hands, fetches the book, points to the word 'potato', one could well lose impetus; the child is no longer interested, although if one carries out the search in a spirit of adventure it *can* be done! A better solution, of course, is to have strips of cardboard with the words written on, in a handy place. But even without this all is not lost. *Anything* in which the child shows interest should be reinforced, first with speech and then with the written word. 'It's a potato. Look, a potato', and a writing with the finger on a flat surface, so that the child can *see* the shape of the letters. Of course it won't go in straight away. Not the first time, not the fiftieth time, but you are giving the child the idea that those peculiar contortions of the mouth are allied to those marks upon the paper or the draining board, and that both imply that object there in your hand.

To look at books together can be a real source of pleasure both for the child and for the parent, and an essential way of encouraging the child to read for himself later. There are, for the very young deaf child, a tremendous number of suitable books on the market, but he needs to share his interest with an adult, not to be left to turn over the pages aimlessly by himself. This sharing can create a very deep bond between parent and child which will prove of inestimable worth later.

I add some comments here on the way to approach this 'reading' together:

1. Try to find some time for it every day.
2. Choose a moment when *he* is likely to be most interested – not when he is tired, not when he's absorbed in something else.

3. Choose a quiet corner, a place where there are no distractions, a place where you can both be comfortable.

4. Choose your book carefully – lots of pictures but good clear simple ones, not overcrowded with detail.

5. Make sure he is wearing a hearing aid. He *should* be wearing it all day long (see Chapter 25) but especially when you are talking to him. If he is profoundly deaf he will not get the consonants but the aid will reinforce the sounds he *can* hear, possibly the vowels, the nasal sounds 'm', 'n', 'ng', and most certainly the rhythm in your voice.

6. Let him turn the pages first and find something which obviously catches his attention – then make him look at you while you tell him what it is. 'That's a *bus*, a big red *bus*. It's going along the road. It's a *bus*.' It isn't the least bit of good saying all that over his head. If he is on your knee, turn his head gently to look at you while you say it. In time he will do it himself automatically. If you are on the floor together, go round in front of him while you say it. The movement will make him realise that you want to tell him something which is really important. And in time his own curiosity, his desperate need to make sense of things, will make him search your face automatically.

7. Don't ever give him single word clues alone. 'Bus', 'train', 'car'. That way, you will bark the words out at him and hinder the development of natural speech. 'It's a bus', 'She's dancing', is always the very least you should say – phrases and sentences, not words alone.

8. Finally don't attempt to read together if you yourself are tired. You need considerable animation in your own voice if the experience is to be a valuable one for you both, and never go on once he begins to lose interest. Two or three short five-minute sessions are likely to be of far more value with a very young child.

A love of books is one of the most valuable things you can give your child. Within those pages lie the answers to many of his problems – understanding the world, making sense of the imperfect patterns he gets from lip-reading, satisfying his curiosity, and providing him with an endless source of both comfort and stimulation.

Chapter Twenty-four

LIP-READING

This chapter should more appropriately be entitled 'Encouraging Speech-Reading' because the term speech-reading is so much more descriptive of the process. It is the whole *face* that the deaf person needs to watch. An expressive face can convey a world of meaning, whereas a deadpan one is of little help. Clues for the deaf person – on meaning, intonation, implied emotion – must come from the whole face, since they cannot come via the ears, and distance from that face is therefore of paramount importance. The position of the face is important too. A profiled face is harder to 'read'. So too is a face set against a distracting background – jazzy curtains, an open door with people passing, a window showing distracting movements outside. All these things need to be borne in mind, and I add the following pointers.

SOME GUIDELINES TO FOLLOW

1. Ensure that there is plenty of light and that it is illuminating you and not him – if your back is to the window then you are in a bad position.
2. Ensure that there is a minimum of distraction in the place where you are trying to talk to him. Is the room in which you are sitting relatively quiet?
3. Are you the right distance away from him? Three to six feet is best, both because of achieving maximum amplification and because he needs to see all your face clearly. Are you on the right level – virtually the same level as he is. One needs when lip-reading to look *slightly* up at people in order to see the teeth and tongue.

4. Ensure that a deaf child is equipped with his hearing aid, and that it is working. This is essential. The deaf child, unlike the deafened adult, does not *have* language; he is not just filling in the gaps, he is actually in the process of *acquiring* language. It is a very difficult process, and he needs every help he can get.

5. Have you cued him in? Does he know what you are talking about in the first place? Is it the book in your hand? Or a comment on the weather?

6. Is the speed with which you are talking right? Are you gabbling? Alternatively are you only giving staccato words and not incorporating the words within sentences so that he has nothing to hold on to in the way of contextual cues?

7. Have you phrased your sentence simply enough? And if he doesn't seem to get it can you rephrase it? Or is it one of the words you have used which he just doesn't know? For example, have you said 'bring' when he only knows 'fetch'? Have you said 'business' when he only knows 'work'?

8. Do you keep your head relatively still or are you always moving it from side to side so that peculiar shadows flit around and make the lip patterns difficult to follow? Do you distort it even more by laughing or chewing while you are speaking, so that essential mouth patterns are entirely lost?

9. Are you distracting him by what you are wearing: clothes with loud strident colours so that he is much more fascinated by following the contours of the stripes, dangling ear-rings that create constant movement, hair which you perpetually brush away from the sides of your face, a beard which you are always plucking, a cigarette which distorts your lips, even sun-glasses, which obscure the expression of your eyes?

10. Are you aware that some sounds of speech – 'h', 'k', 'g', 'ng', are completely invisible? That others are indistinguishable – that 'map' could just as easily be 'pop', that 'ten' could just as easily be 'dead'.

Lip-reading is rather like crossword solving; one is very dependent upon clues. And the fewer distractions a deaf person has to contend with at the same time, the more likely are his chances of success. In addition, of course, a relaxed situation, not one fraught with tension, is far more conducive to good results. Confidence on your part that the outcome will be favourable is all-important. If you approach the situation tentatively there will be anxiety in your voice and tension in your mouth. He needs *you* to be the extrovert, to give all you can. To appreciate his problems you have only to switch on the TV without any sound at all, *before* you know what the programme is about. This will give an indication of the problems which a deaf person faces all the time.

Chapter Twenty-five

THE HEARING AID

There are three parts to a hearing aid:

1. Microphone – which receives sound waves (mechanical energy) and converts them into electrical energy.
2. Amplifier – which amplifies that energy.
3. Receiver – which converts that electrical energy back into mechanical energy.

For a hearing aid to be effective, three things must be right:

1. Gain – whether the *amount* of amplification which takes place is sufficient.
2. Frequency response – whether the *frequencies* (pitch) of the sounds amplified are the correct ones for that particular person.
3. Output – whether the sound eventually passed on to the ear is loud enough (i.e. whether what goes in, plus the amplification which takes place, is adequate).

The provision of hearing aids has altered radically in the last four years. It is vital that a deaf child should be provided with the best possible aid. Prescription of an aid is not a 'one off' event. Frequent revision is necessary; what may seem the best aid at 18 months (when precise diagnosis is difficult) is not necessarily so at five years, or again at 15 years.

1. Commercial aids are available if the DHSS range is unsuitable.
2. Not only the aid, but also the lead, ear-mould and receiver need to be repeatedly checked for efficiency.

3. The lead should be of a length suitable for the child; leads that are too long will cause problems.
4. The ear-mould should fit closely and not whistle; soft acrylic vinyl or silicone rubber ear-moulds are most desirable for comfort.
5. The receiver and cord must be the matching one for that aid, otherwise it will be useless. And it must not be too heavy for a small child, otherwise it will drag the ear-mould out of the ear.
6. The batteries powering the aid must always be at peak efficiency.
7. For teenagers – for psychological and cosmetic reasons – a post-aural aid (one worn behind the ear) may be preferred, but post-aural aids are not always as powerful as body-worn aids.

For more technical details concerning hearing aids and their use, the following books and articles will be helpful:

Holsgrove, G. J. (1979). *The Selection of Personal Hearing Aids for Children*. (Reprints available from the Divisional Education Office, The Grange, High Street, Stevenage, Hertfordshire SG1 3BD.)

Nolan, M. and Tucker, G. (1981). *The Hearing Impaired Child and the Family*. Human Horizons Series. Souvenir Press, London.

The Teacher of the Deaf (1983).

Fitting and evaluating aids, **7**, 3.

Radio aids, **7**, 4.

Auxiliary aids, **7**, 5.

How do children manage with grown-up hearing aids, **8**, 4.

(This is the Journal of the British Association of Teachers of the Deaf.)

WHAT DOES A DEAF CHILD HEAR THROUGH A HEARING AID?

Obviously no two deaf children are identical. What they can hear may vary enormously:

1. It will depend on which particular nerve cells are damaged. It is more usual for the higher frequencies to be missing .

2. It will depend on the quality of the deaf child's hearing aid and on whether this is functioning at optimum level, and also on the quality and fit of the ear-mould.
3. It will depend on how much *practice* the deaf child has had in listening.
4. It will depend on psychological factors.

WHAT ARE THE EASIEST SOUNDS FOR A DEAF CHILD TO HEAR?

There are three important properties of sound:

1. *Duration* is how long a sound lasts.
2. *Intensity* is the *power* of a sound, and is expressed in decibels (e.g. the sound pressure of a jet plane is approximately 120 decibels, conversational speech is approximately 60 decibels, heavy traffic is midway between the two).
3. *Frequency* is concerned with *vibration*. Anything which vibrates (e.g. a stringed instrument, a glass set in motion by a singer) does so at a certain number of times per second. Frequency is expressed in hertz (Hz). 1000 cycles of vibration per second = 1000Hz. The frequencies on a piano range from 27.5Hz up to 4186Hz. Frequency is similar to pitch.

The human ear *may* hear sounds between 20Hz and 20 000Hz but it hears most easily sounds between 500Hz and 4000Hz, i.e. sounds in the *middle range*. The *sounds of speech* are almost all within this middle range, i.e. 500Hz – 4000Hz.

The sounds of speech also have varying amounts of *intensity*, e.g. 'aw' as in 'fork' is the strongest sound. It is 30 times stronger than 'th' as in 'thin'. This means that a deaf child will hear it much more easily. In general, most of the vowel sounds are strong, whereas the consonants are weak. 'ar' (*f*ather), 'oa' (*b*oat), 'oo' (*sh*oe), 'ee' (*three*) are easier to hear than *f*eather, *s*ea, or *p*in. The nasal sounds m, n, ng are somewhere in the middle.

Unfortunately, although we *hear* the vowels more easily, it is not the vowels, but the consonants which make speech easier to understand:

If a deaf child hears only:

    air   oo   ee-oo   i?

he will not find it easy to understand, and yet even with the best hearing aid in the world this may be all he does hear. If only he could hear the *consonants* instead of the vowels, he would have a much better chance of understanding, because consonants would give him:

	Whar	dar	yar	larve?
or				
	Wher	der	yer	lerve?

and he would be able to guess at the meaning. It is most unlikely, however, that he *will* hear the consonants, and therefore intelligent guesses are denied to him.

WHAT A HEARING AID CAN AND CANNOT DO

It does not give a deaf child automatic hearing. Putting a hearing aid on a deaf baby is not the same as putting it on an adult who has gone partially deaf. The adult already knows what speech is, he knows that words have meaning. When you give a deaf adult a hearing aid it makes the speech, which was quiet and therefore difficult to decipher before, a great deal clearer, and the deaf adult understands better. When you put a hearing aid on a deaf child of one year who has never heard, all he hears is a noise in which some sounds are louder than others, but none of which have any meaning. Perhaps it is rather like us standing in a shop in Moscow and putting on a hearing aid. There would be lots of loud noises, but we wouldn't at first know what they meant. Then we might associate a certain 'ping' with the cash register, but all those voices going on around us would have no meaning at all. But even so we should be better off than the deaf baby, because we should know that the people round us were communicating, saying things, asking things, giving out information. A deaf baby has to learn first of all what speech is: that the sounds he hears, together with the contortions of the mouth, express certain meanings.

The hearing aid will help him to the following extent:

1. It will prevent him from being utterly cut off. He will not need to live in a world of silence. He will hear loud noises such as a door banging or a shrieking siren. More importantly

he will hear when somebody is trying to talk to him and he may look up. And only in that way will he be ready to lip-read.

2. He will probably hear the rhythms of speech, and this will help him to develop a pleasing and modulated voice of his own. The aid may also give him certain clues as to the message given – whether it is a command, a statement or a question.

3. He may hear certain vowels – 'ar', 'aw', 'oo' for instance, and if he is less deaf the nasal consonants 'm', 'n', 'ng'.

4. If he is only partially hearing and not profoundly deaf he may hear quite a lot of the 'quieter' consonants through a hearing aid: 'f', 't', 's', for instance.

But this book is concerned, not with the partially hearing, but with the severely and profoundly deaf – and they do not like the term, still unfortunately in current use, 'deaf and *dumb*'. To be dumb implies stupidity, and stupid they most certainly are not. I have known some very clever deaf people, whose potential was indeed very great, if only it could have been realised. Neither are the deaf 'dumb' in the sense of having no voice. In almost all cases there is nothing the matter with the speech mechanism itself; it is simply that the loss of the sense of hearing denies them the ability to modify their voice, to know when it is loud and raucous, or high and screeching, and they are, therefore, unable to imitate the speech which we all hear around us. It *can* be done by the deafest of individuals, but only by consistent effort and only by struggling from the very earliest years.

THE IMPORTANCE OF A HEARING AID

Hardly any child is so deaf that a hearing aid is useless.

He may not hear what you say through it, but it will give him clues.

He needs to wear it *consistently*, every day, all the day, to get the most benefit – if he broke a leg and the hospital gave him crutches you wouldn't give him the crutches one day and take them away the next; he'd need to practise all the time.

If you assume he's going to wear an aid he'll think it's a natural thing to do too.

When he's young he'll need help in stopping it from being a nuisance. Make a secure harness for it. If it falls out when he's crawling or playing, he won't like it.

Make sure it's kept clean and hasn't got food or dirt in it.

Check it two or three times a day to make sure it's working. Does it need a new battery? Is the lead broken? Is the ear-mould blocked with wax? Teach him to look after it himself, to wash the mould regularly, to put it in a safe place at night.

When he's older he'll need help in disguising it, so that other people don't remark on it. Make sure that if he gets an ear-level aid, then it's one that is powerful enough for him.

If your child starts wearing a hearing aid when he's very young, then he'll accept it all the more easily, and he'll realise *for himself* just how valuable it is.

Even if he can only hear a tiny amount through it, even that is valuable:

1. He will hear himself chattering and that will help him to develop a more natural voice.
2. He will know when you say something, and when he looks up he'll be ready to lip-read you when you say it again.
3. He will hear the rhythm of your voice and will be better able to imitate it.
4. He may hear some of the louder sounds – the vowel sounds – and he may be able to imitate them.

Chapter Twenty-six

HELPING YOUR CHILD TO TALK

THE IMPORTANCE OF MUSIC

I suppose the most worrying thing for the parents of a deaf child is whether that child will ever be able to talk in the normal way. Perhaps it is better to state at the outset that there will always be an element of deafness in the speech, however good the training, however good the hearing aid, but that does not mean it need be unintelligible, nor need it be unpleasant to listen to. The speech of foreigners, of English people who have a strong dialect, is not unattractive, it is different, that is all, and our listening ears must make allowances. What is, however, all important, is the *musicality* of voice, its varieties of pitch; we need gentleness not harshness, depth and resonance not screeching, and much of this depends on the training received in the very earliest years. This is something in which parents can help from the moment the deafness is discovered.

1. Make sure your child has the best possible aid for his degree of deafness. Don't think that the important thing is to hide the aid away from curious eyes. It isn't. The most important thing is to see that the child receives amplification of sound all his waking life – how else is he to become aware of sound itself – to learn to differentiate as far as he is able? He *must* learn that sound is important, that sound has meaning, and that sound is to be enjoyed.

   Let him listen to all the normal sounds around the house: the door bell, the alarm clock, the toilet flushing, someone knocking on the door, the dog barking. He may be able to hear some of them with his aid.

2. Make time every day for the *enjoyment* of sound. Put on the radio or record player and dance with your eight-month-old in your arms or hold hands with your two-year-old. You can't tell what he will actually hear, perhaps very little, but you are helping him by the rhythm of your body; you are showing him that rhythm is a part of life. It is a mistake to think that only the things which he can *see* are important to a deaf child. What he can *feel* is vitally important too, and he will feel sounds and music through his body.

3. At the same time, try to discover which sounds seem to give your child the most pleasure. Is it the deep notes of the organ or the shrill cry of a whistle? Does he like the thud of the drum or the twang of a string? And should any sound ever seem to cause him pain or distress, never expose him to it if you can avoid it. (For instance the hoot of the diesel, entering the tunnels on the journey to Leeds, sometimes caused Judith to cry, but once I was aware of this I would turn the volume on the hearing aid down when I knew the tunnels were approaching, putting it up again later.)

4. When he is a little older teach him to listen. Get someone to help you by banging a drum, and show him that every time he hears it he can jump forward. Let him do it first when he can see the drum, and then encourage him not to watch, but to listen. If you make it a game, he will love it, and will learn to concentrate, to focus his attention on what he can hear. Or you can try it with the radio. Every time you switch it on he is to run round the room. When you turn it off, he must stand still. This way he will learn the difference between when there is sound and when there is not.

5. Later on, try to find out if he can distinguish between high notes and low notes. If you have a piano, this is much easier. Let him stand near it while you play the low notes. Then tell him that it's low, near the ground, and he must crouch down when he hears it. Then play the high notes and show him that these are high, and he must jump up, up in the air when he hears them. Let him do this lots of

times while he watches you play. Then let him try *without* watching you, just by listening, and see if he can do it then. But if he can't, never mind. Bring him back to watch you again; never let him lose confidence in himself.

6. Let him clap out rhythms with you. It will help if you sing at the same time: Mum-*my*, Dad-*dy*, Jon-a-*than*, Re-*bec*-ca. Later on, when he is older, try covering up your mouth, and sing words of one, two or three syllables and see if he can tell you how many there are. But never force him, always make it fun.

7. Help him to distinguish between different kinds of tempo: marching and swaying, for example. This is where hearing children can help, pretending to be soldiers when the music is a marching tune, or holding scarves and swaying gently like the branches of a tree when you play a waltz melody. Let him watch what they are doing and join in, and then see if he can tell the difference when he is on his own with you.

All of these suggestions can be started at any age – as young as eight months or at any time through childhood. You don't have to be an expert to help your child in this way. Nobody could have known less than I did about the nature of sound at the time of Judith's birth, and yet I believe that the efforts I made in encouraging her to be aware of sound and rhythm, were of crucial importance in the development of her speech.

THE DEVELOPMENT OF SPEECH

Just as you can help your child's voice quality through music, so you do not have to be a trained teacher of the deaf to encourage the early imitation of speech. The first thing to appreciate is the importance of breath. No speech sound stands in isolation. It is connected to those in front of it and those behind it – one does not speak in jerks – 'b-oa-t' for instance. The sounds are all joined together, the position of the one determines the length of another; a 'b' at the beginning of a word is of different length from a 'b' at the end of a word, and both are affected by adjoining vowels. It is clues from the *length* of sounds which assist intelligibility, but for a deaf child to produce a sequence of sounds of the correct length, he *must* have a sustained flow of breath. If he does not have this flow of breath, then he will not be able to give the greater length to those consonants which demand it – 's' and 'f', 'm' and 'ng' for instance. If he clips them, then his speech will become far less intelligible to the outsider, and if his lack of breath is such that he barks out single words instead of speaking, as hearing people do, in phrases and sentences, then his voice will be less intelligible still.

Breath, then, is very important; you need to make absolutely certain that he can control the flow.

1. Is he relaxed? Nobody can breathe properly if they are all tensed up (tighten your shoulder and stomach muscles and see how impossible it is to breathe properly). If he's not relaxed then you can't start. Make sure that what you are doing is in the nature of a game.

2. Is his nose clear? No one can breathe properly with a stuffed-up nose.

3. Can he blow? Blow a feather or a ping-pong ball across a table? Blow talcum powder off your hand? Blow a plastic windmill? Blow bits of tissue paper you hold in your mouth? Blow a candle flame gently, so that it bends but doesn't go out?

4. Can he close his mouth properly? Let him watch you in a mirror, opening and shutting your mouth. If he can't close his properly, then perhaps he is using it to breathe with, instead of breathing through his nose. If he continues to do this he will find it difficult later to say the nasal consonants, especially 'm'.

5. Can he suck? Sucking helps to round the lips. 'Oo' and 'wh' will depend on this later.

6. Can he lick? The tongue needs to be very mobile. (Its correct position will be very important later when he wants to say 'l' and 'r', 't' and 'n'.) Can he put his tongue out in all kinds of positions? Can he make it go up and down, side to side, all the way round his open mouth? Make a game of it. Look in the mirror.

7. Can he imitate the shapes your mouth is making? Let him feel your face as you say 'oo'. Let him look in the mirror and try to copy you as you say 'ar' and 'ee'. But let him feel *your* face; don't handle his, or he may resent it. Collect pictures of

different faces saying these sounds. Stick them up and see if he's interested enough to imitate them. But *never* distort your mouth unduly. Never *over*-emphasise, or he will acquire bad habits which will take years to eradicate.

8. Can he imitate the noises which animals make – 'woof-woof', 'baa-aa'. Try making the sound holding a toy animal in your hand (or a picture if you haven't got the toy) and say 'The dog says woof-woof', 'The sheep says baa-aa'.

If you try out all these suggestions then you will be really helping your child. It doesn't need superhuman intelligence on either your part or his, but it does need time – a few minutes every day. It can also be tremendous fun for both of you, and you will be laying the best possible foundations for a natural speaking voice.

JUST TALKING

The preceding two sections contained suggestions as to what you might do with your child to help him in the very early days to acquire a pleasant voice and to acquire control over his flow of breath and mouth movements. I believe that both are very important, and both, unfortunately, are often neglected. However, it is even more important to treat your child as a normal hearing baby and to speak to him as such. You must talk to him all the time, even though there is no response, even though he just appears to stare back at you. The mother of a hearing baby automatically talks to him, however young he is. She approaches his cot when she hears him crying, talking as she goes. 'Now then, what's the matter? Is it dinner time then? Come along. Mummy lift you up. Up we come. There, that's better, isn't it? Come along, let's go and find your dinner.' The words may vary, but the patter is usually there. She goes on talking even though the baby can't understand a word, and by so doing she creates a bond between herself and the child which is reinforced over and over again as the day progresses. A deaf child needs this bond even more. He may never hear the words, but he will gradually become aware that the face that looms over his cot, the smile that enlightens the face, the mouth that moves into different shapes as he watches it, the body that hugs him close, are all trying to tell him something, and because, in his infinite curiosity, he really wants to know, he will try all the harder to look for cues as to meaning.

A deaf baby should be talked to all the time, as you dress and undress him, as you support him in the bath, as you feed him, as you put him into his pram. The routine things you do are particularly important, because you can use the same words over and over again. It is your repetition of these words, when he is one or two years old, which are going to engrave them for ever on his memory. No school, even the very best of nursery schools, is ever going to have the chances that you have, to talk about the bath and the soap, and his little boat and his knees that need scrubbing. No school will ever have the thousands of opportunities that you have, to talk about his blue hat and his brown shoes and his buttons – 1, 2, 3, 4, 5 – that have to be fastened so many times. No school will know about his favourite bunny rabbit with its floppy ears, his mug with the picture of the pussy on it. But you know, and you can talk about them all the time, every day, every time you bath him, every time you put his things on to go to the shops, every time you get his dinner ready. It may not be easy. It takes a lot more time to wait to get his attention and talk to him as you put his coat on, instead of just pushing him into it. You're busy enough, and you've all the shopping to do, and you want to get on. But in those five years before he goes to school you can achieve so much, and those five years can never be relived.

You may think to yourself, 'but I'm not a talkative person, it doesn't come naturally to me to talk to an unresponsive deaf baby.' If it is any comfort to you, nor was I, and it didn't come naturally to me either. But I did it, because I could see the sense in doing it once it was pointed out to me. Never underrate yourself. Sometimes the quieter mum is the more sensitive one, the one who watches her child all the time. She sees what he is interested in and chooses that moment to talk about it. She doesn't gabble words over his head. She watches intently to see when he looks up at her and *then* she says something.

SOME POINTS TO REMEMBER

1. Have faith in yourself, that what you are doing is going to work, even if it takes a long time.

2. As much as you can, follow his interests. Wait until he picks up the carrot to tell him what it is. It will register more if he's shown an interest in the first place.

3. But at the same time, try and *arouse* his interest by talking about what *you* are doing as you do it. For example, you can talk to him all the time you are washing up or baking, if he's watching you. Or you can push a toy car along the floor and give a running commentary: 'Here's a blue car. Look, it's going along the road, round the corner. Oh look, now it's going up, up over the bridge, down the bridge and through the tunnel.' The one thing you mustn't do is take *his* car, the one he was playing with before you grabbed it, or he'll resent it. What child wouldn't!

4. When you're talking to him, try and make sure that your face is in the light. If he doesn't seem to be very interested, could it be because your back is to the window, and he can't lip-read you properly? By just moving a bit to the side, you could well get his interest back again.

5. Is his hearing aid working properly? Are you sure his mould isn't blocked by wax? Or his microphone smeared with chocolate? That his lead is firmly fixed? That his mould is in his ear? That his aid is switched on?

6. Always be very clear in showing him what you are talking about. With a young child you need to have some object there, ready at hand, a ball, his coat, some sweets. He has to have a clue first. Even if you think he can lip-read 'Daddy' – and he probably can, if Daddy is there – he won't expect you to be talking about Daddy when you're bending over the cooker, and he'll probably think you're trying to tell him something about the cooker or the pan, when what you might have said is, 'Daddy will be home soon, we'll put the dinner on.' The abstract, the thing that isn't there, is very, very difficult for a deaf child. He needs to be aware of it, yes, or his imagination will never grow, his powers of reasoning will never develop. But right at the beginning, when he is

struggling to make sense of words, he has to see the connection between the word on your lips and the object nearby. He has to make the connection between that thing you have in your hand – say an apple – and the movement of your jaws, lips and tongue as you say it. He has to build up gradually, oh so gradually, a vocabulary of words that mean something, on which he can rely to make sense of life. And every word added, every meaning grasped, is like another bit of cement added to the foundations, on which he can build in the future.

7. Use plenty of action words when you're talking to him. It's much easier to teach him 'bus', 'car' and 'train' than to teach him 'giving', 'choosing' and 'putting', but they are equally important concepts. So often a deaf child knows the names of all kinds of objects but doesn't know that he can push and pull, stir and rub, pour and roll, shake and press and squeeze. Even the word 'make' is one he is often unaware of, and yet how often do we use it at home – making the beds, making a cake, making a meal, etc. You will have to act them out, time and again: sitting, standing, running, hopping, skipping, falling, climbing, lifting, dancing. If you are clever you can draw them too, using stick men. If you can't draw, look for pictures in magazines of people doing different things – 'Oh look, she's cleaning her teeth, brushing her hair, he's shaving, the girl's eating, the boy's drinking.' Get all your friends and relations on the look-out too to spot pictures for you, cut them out and save them for you to stick in a book that you can look at often. In the same way, look for pictures of people or things that illustrate 'up', 'down', 'through', 'under', 'over', 'in', 'on'. And you can act these out all the time: Teddy's *in* the box, Dolly's *under* the chair, the train's going *through* the tunnel. Put the red brick *near* the yellow one. Lay the forks *on* the table. Draw attention to colours and sizes and shapes – a green plate, a red shoe, a blue and white jumper, a big elephant, a long snake, a round ball.

There are so many things around you all the time, so many things that you will meet naturally in the course of each day, that you need never fear that you will be short of opportunities.

Some helpful suggestions for stimulating language development are given in:

Nolan, M. and Tucker, G. (1981). *The Hearing Impaired Child and the Family*. Human Horizon Series. Souvenir Press, London.

ADDITIONAL SOURCES OF INFORMATION

Reading

Robbins, Carol and Robbins, Clive (1980). *Music for the Hearing Impaired: Music, Special Education, Music Therapy, Hearing and Deaf*. Magnamusic-Baton Inc, 10370 Page Industrial Boulevard, St Louis, Missouri 63132.

Uden, A. Van (1977). *A World of Language for Deaf Children*. Swets Publishing Service, The Netherlands.

Video cassettes

Claus Bang's Music Therapy Programme with English commentary.

Claus Bang's Stereo Cassette Tapes.

(Obtainable from Head of Music Therapy Training, Claus Bang, Aalborgskolen, Kollegievej 1, DK 9210 Aalborg SØ.)

Chapter Twenty-seven

ENCOURAGING MEMORY

For the deaf child a good memory is especially important, and yet it is extraordinarily difficult to cultivate. We hear speech through our ears all the time, words, phrases, sentences are constantly repeated and reinforced. Even though we talk as much as we can to our deaf children, they are still getting an imperfect pattern on the lips, and it is a fleeting pattern that is difficult to remember, far more difficult than remembering something heard through one's ears. Visual patterns are vitally important to a deaf child and any game which helps him to look carefully and intently at something is to be encouraged.

When Judith was very young we played a lot of games with her that involved *matching* – colours, objects, shapes. For all of these, she had to look very carefully. Later on we used the picture lotto cards every day, and if she was bored with sitting we made a physical exercise of it, and I hid the cards round the room or even round the house.

Within a year or two we started on Pelmanism and I believe this helped her powers of concentration enormously. We would sort out about five pairs of numbers from a pack of cards, mix up the 10 cards and turn them face downwards on the floor. Then we would take it in turns to lift up a card, look at it, and if, say, it were a five, turn over another card, looking for its twin. If we were unlucky, then both cards were replaced face down in exactly the same positions. If we got two alike, then we removed them and they counted as our 'score'. Judith became an expert in remembering where each card was, and rapidly made up her pairs. From five pairs we progressed to 10 pairs, and eventually to using the whole pack. We played it for hours, sometimes just the two of us, sometimes with the whole family, and it undoubtedly did a great deal for her powers of concentration.

Another game we used when she was about five, was Kim's Game, where about 10 familiar objects – a cup, a spoon, a Teddy bear, etc. were laid on a tray. She had a few minutes to look at them, then I took the tray away, took one of the objects off, and put the tray back in front of her. She had to look carefully and tell me which one was missing. This was a good game to play when other children were present, because they could take turns in removing an article from the tray, and if the remaining children all had a piece of paper, they could then draw the missing object, even if they couldn't write it.

Later still, we taught her many card games, particularly ones like Happy Families, Rummy, Newmarket, Bezique and eventually Bridge, in all of which she had to remember who held which card.

All these, I believe, are a help towards encouraging concentration and short-term memory, but long-term memory must be encouraged too. Judith's long-term memory seemed particularly poor. She could not remember, as her brother and sister could at the same age, places we had been to, or people we had seen, and we found it very necessary to collect as many photographs as we could of both people and places and to bring them out often and talk about them. In later years she would take delight in doing this for herself; the visual record seemed to be essential to fix the event in her mind.

From the earliest years I used nursery rhymes to help her with her speech, but once she started piano lessons I realised just how important the sequence of sounds was becoming, and I began to teach her rhymes and jingles in earnest, in order, again, to help her with her memory.

Rhymes mean little to deaf children, since the *sound* of words is very hard for them to appreciate, but nevertheless they can get a lot of enjoyment from jingles, which are short, easy to memorise, and have a sense of rhythm:

> Two red apples
> On the tree
> One for you
> And one for me.

Please come to my house,
To my house,
To my house,
Please come to my house,
And have a cup of tea.

RHYMES AND JINGLES CAN HELP SPEECH TOO

There are some 42 sounds in the English language, and by devising a short jingle to fit each sound it is possible to find out whether a child can in fact produce that sound satisfactorily. Some examples follow:

'aw'

Bill and Paul
Each had a ball
And they threw their ball
Right over the wall.

'oo'

If you could choose
Some new shoes,
Would you have blue
Or would black do?

'ie'

I like to go for a hike
To stride for miles
And climb the stiles.

's'

Seven smooth snakes
Slithering along
S–s–s–s
Goes their snaking song.

'u'

My mother suddenly said to us
You must hustle and bustle to catch the bus
Now hurry along and don't make a fuss
If we're going to Granny's we must catch the bus.

'th'

There's my Mother,
There's my Dad,
There's my brother,
Now I'm glad.

'w'

Which way shall we walk?
Which way's best?
We'll walk this way
But who wants a rest?

'k'

Cabbage and cauliflower,
Carrots and peas
Cook them carefully
Catherine please.

'ch'

Cheese and chicken
Chops and chips
I'd choose them all
If I were rich.

The above are only jingles, but they can usefully be employed:

To decide whether a child is saying a certain sound correctly.
To give him pleasure in repeating it once it is fixed.
To help his memory for a sequence of sounds.
To help him maintain a good flow of breath.
To lead him on to better things!

From the above jingles a deaf child can progress quite naturally to learning some of the many delightful poems in the books listed below. Learning poetry can be great fun, and it will help a deaf child because:

It is rhythmic.
It is written in short lines.
It is easy to remember.
The words are often simple and idiomatic.
It is often funny.
It often tells a story.
It helps imagination, because it creates a vivid picture in one's mind.

In addition to poetry, an older deaf child can be helped to increase his powers of memory in the following ways:

1. Card games, as above. *Board* games – ludo, draughts, etc., are useful for *social* training but card games are best for *memory* training.
2. Repeating sequences of numbers – e.g. working up from 5–7–3–4 to strings of seven, eight or nine numbers.
3. Repeating short but meaningful sentences – e.g. 'I went to the park yesterday and played cricket with my friends.'
4. Playing the old favourite party game: 'I went on holiday and I took – my umbrella, my suitcase, two pairs of jeans, etc. etc.' Or 'I took my shopping bag and I put in it: some apples, some bananas, some carrots, etc.'
5. Learning a role in a short dialogue – e.g. At the doctor's:

DOCTOR: Good morning. Sit down. What's the trouble?
PATIENT: I've got a very sore throat.
DOCTOR: Let's have a look, shall we. Say 'ar'. Oh yes. It looks a bit red. Have you got a bad cough too?

PATIENT: Just a little bit.

DOCTOR: I see. Well, I'll give you a prescription for some tablets. Take them three times a day, after meals, for a week. If your throat still isn't any better then come back and see me.

PATIENT: Thank you very much. Goodbye.

Children enjoy acting out little scenes such as these. It gives them confidence in speaking, it helps their memory, it can be great fun, and it will probably lead them on to making up their own.

To train their deaf child's memory is yet another way in which parents can help to give him a valuable start in life.

SOME SUGGESTED BOOKS

Carr, S. (1982). *Birds, Beasts and Fishes*. Batsford Limited, London.

Cole, W. (1975). *Beastly Boys and Ghastly Girls*. Methuen Children's Books, London.

Corrin, Sara and Corrin, Stephen (eds) (1982), *Once Upon A Rhyme*. Faber and Faber, London.

Elson, D. (1979). *If You Should Meet a Crocodile*. World's Work Limited. (Windmill Press, Kingswood, Tadworth KT20 6TG)

Farjeon, E. (1981). *Invitation to a Mouse and Other Poems*. Pelham Books, London.

Nash, O. and Blake, Q. (1979). *Custard and Company*. Kestrel Books, London.

Palmer, G. and Lloyd, N. (1973). *Round About Six*. Frederick Warne Limited, London.

Palmer, G. and Lloyd, N. (1972). *Round About Eight*. Frederick Warne Limited, London.

Palmer, G. and Lloyd, N. (1976). *Round About Nine*. Frederick Warne Limited, London.

Palmer, G. and Lloyd, N. (1979). *Round About Ten*. Frederick Warne Limited, London.

Wilson, R. (ed) (1977). *Time's Delight*. Hamlyn Publishing Group, London.

Chapter Twenty-eight

THE OLDER DEAF CHILD

This book is written primarily to tell the general public something of what deafness implies, and to help those with a deaf baby who are just beginning on the long uphill struggle. For those who have an older deaf child the picture is a different one. They have lived through the struggles of the early years, they know all too well just how many things can go wrong, they have accepted the deafness as fact, but they are in danger now of assuming that there is nothing else that they can do. To keep on continually talking to one's child, to keep on trying to provide new experiences and to explain them to him, becomes less and less easy. It is so much more peaceful to sit together in front of the TV assuming that because he sits there with you and gazes at the screen with rapt attention he is thereby getting the same benefits that you are. He may enjoy the cartoons, the action, the blood and thunder, but how much of the story can he follow? How much information is he getting? Dare you ask him, to find out? Can you forgo your own enjoyment to explain what the cowboy said? Or why everybody laughed? Or what country they are talking about?

Subtitling may make it easier for some children, but only if they can read the subtitles, and unfortunately the deaf are usually several years retarded in this, due to the immense difficulties of acquiring language in the first place. Have you tried to find books from the library that he will be able to read for himself? So often I have seen books given to a deaf child by well-meaning relatives that are totally unsuitable. The language structure is far too difficult; the child never gets past the first paragraph. And now the deaf child is in a Catch 22 situation. He needs to read, to enlarge his general knowledge of the world around him, and to increase his knowledge of words. But he can't read and find out, because the language of the books is too difficult for him, and puts him off. You can help him by going to the library and showing him how to choose books that make sense, that he can understand. You can help him by going through them with him and explaining any new words.

You can help him too by sitting down at home and talking. And then writing down some of what you've said, using speech balloons, because that way he'll absorb some normal idiomatic language. What you have written will make sense, because it was part of a normal conversation. Sometimes comics will help in this way too, but very often they won't, because the speech balloons, even in comics, have phrases such as, 'hasn't a clue', 'no chance', 'we'll clobber you', which he will not know.

So often, parents, once their deaf children get to adolescence, assume that there is nothing more they can do; that the children are in good hands at school, and that all the learning will take place there. But the deaf child has five or six waking hours at home during each school day, almost as long as his time in school, and much, much more when account is taken of weekends and holidays. He needs to use that time to build up his own resources for the future. Reading is a valuable one, because it will provide him with information. The more he reads the more he will find out. The more he finds out, the wider his horizons will become. But he needs your help if he is to find his way through the maze of books. It is much, much easier to get him a home computer and turn him loose with that. He will probably play quite happily for hours and he will certainly increase his mathematical skills, and probably his powers of reasoning too. But it won't help him to find out about the world. It won't help him to be any less isolated. It won't give him the warmth of human companionship.

Just as reading will enlarge his mental horizons, so the ability to play games will help his social development. Football is fine when he is younger. But unless he's an outstanding player, he is going to find it hard to carry it on once he leaves school. He will need to know games suitable for one or two players. Tennis and squash, badminton and bowls, darts and snooker. Is there a club near at hand where he can get a smattering of all these? Can you teach him card games at home – whist, solo, bridge, or the most popular board games – draughts, chess, ludo, Scrabble, Monopoly? The more things he knows, the easier he will find it to 'fit in' with other people; the more likely he will be to find a buddy at work to share interests with.

What about other clubs and societies? – Scouts, Guides, Boys' Brigade, St John Ambulance? I have known deaf boys and girls who have belonged to all these and who have mixed on equal terms in them with hearing children. It was not easy for any of them at first, and they needed their parents to take the initial steps, but with understanding, on the one side, perseverance on the other, and good humour on both, remarkable things were achieved. A deaf child needs a solid core of confidence within himself. As he grows older he *knows* that he sounds funny when he talks, he knows that people often can't make out what he says and he can't understand them either, but if he can say, 'Well, I can beat you at this', or 'I'm as good as you are at that', and, better still, 'I'll *show* you how to play that', then he's well on the way to becoming truly integrated.

Don't put all your energies into worrying what kind of a job he is going to get when he leaves school. Nobody can plan five or ten years ahead. Open up as many avenues as you can for him *now*. That way you will provide him with inner resources for the future which will stand him in good stead. To accept deafness for one's child is never easy; to go on accepting it is perhaps harder still. You don't envisage the situations that are going to arise, you don't realise that for a 10-year-old it is desperately hard not to understand the joke that everyone else in the family has heard and is laughing about. You don't realise that for a 16-year-old it is desperately hard not to acquire a boy- or girlfriend easily. You see, perhaps, that the goals you aimed at for your child are becoming impossible to attain, and you have to readjust. Each time your child enters a new phase – going to school, moving house, starting work – you suffer with him in what you know he will encounter. Misunderstandings, isolation, ignorance. Each time the family is gathered together, and particularly at festive occasions – birthdays, weddings, Christmas – you realise all over again the depth of his isolation. I doubt if the parent of any handicapped child is ever free from a sense of responsibility; from an awareness of the child's suffering.

But to state that, is only to acknowledge the problem. What matters is the efforts we as parents make towards accepting it, and in trying to find a positive solution. The following article is written by a parent of four children, two of whom are hearing-impaired:

Paget, S. (1983). Long-term grieving in parents of hearing-impaired children: A synthesis of parental experience. *The Teacher of the Deaf*, May edition. (Reprints available from Mrs R McAree, 96 High Street, Boston Spa, Wetherby, West Yorkshire LS23 6DB.)

SELECTED BOOKS FOR THE OLDER DEAF CHILD

For the older deaf child who finds reading difficult the following books, or series of books, are helpful. In most cases they are listed by publisher.

FICTION

Publisher: Hutchinson Books Limited, 17–21 Conway Street, London W1P 6JD. The *Bulls Eye* Series which includes abbreviated modern stories such as: *Jaws, The Dam Busters, The Day of the Jackal, Doctor No, The Triffids, Diamonds are Forever.*

Publisher: Longmans, 5 Bentinck Street, London W1M 5RN. *New Method Supplementary Readers*, Stages 1–5. These include abbreviated classics.
Structural Readers. These have simplified vocabulary and structure. The titles include abbreviated classics and other stories for use with children between the age of 8–12, 12–15, and 15+.

Publisher: Ernest Benn Limited, Sovereign Way, Tonbridge, Kent TN9 1RW.
The *Inner Ring Sports* Series.

Publisher: E. J. Arnold and Sons Limited, Parkside, Dewsbury Road, Leeds LS11 5TD.
Patches Series.
Sea Hawk Books.
Flightpath to Reading Books.
Griffin Pirate Stories.

Publisher: Hart-Davis Educational Limited (Granada Publishing Limited, 8 Grafton Street, London W1X 3LA).
Hurricane Series; *First Folk Tales*; *Second Folk Tales*; and others.

Publisher: Ginn and Company Limited, Prebendal House, Parson's Fee, Aylesbury, Bucks HP20 2QZ.
Trend Series. These have very simplified language and structure and are suitable for teenagers.
Very easy-to-read stories such as: *Shorty the Puppy*, *Young Shorty Books*, *More Young Shorty Books*, *Young Shorty Again*, *Rescue Stories*, *More Rescue Stories*, *Rescue Adventures*.

Publisher: Thomas Nelson & Sons Limited, Mayfield Road, Walton-on-Thames, Surrey KT12 5PL.
Very easy-to-read stories such as *Help Stories*, *Help Yourself* Series.

NON-FICTION

Transport

Publisher: Macdonald Publishers Limited, Maxwell House, 74 Worship Street, London EC2A 2EN.
The *Macdonald Starters* Series has a large range of titles in a simplified format.
The *Macdonald Easy Reading* Series with titles including: *Cars*; *Trains*; *Ships*.
Macdonald Whizz Kids Series including *Bikes*.

Nature

Publisher: Usborne Publishing, 20 Garrick Street, London WC2E 9BJ.
Titles including *Understanding Cats* by B. Gibb and *Understanding Dogs* by S. Swallow.

Publisher: Latimer House Limited, 74 Worship Street, London EC2A 2EN.
Explorer Guides Series including *Dogs*; *Birds*; *Horses and Ponies*; *Shells*, and other titles.

Publisher: Hamish Hamilton Limited, 57–9 Long Acre, London WC2E 9JZ.

The *A Closer Look At* Series including *Ants*; *Dogs*; *Birds*; *Deserts*; *Great Cats*.

Publisher: Wayland Publishers Limited, 49 Lansdowne Place, Hove, Sussex BN3 1HF.

Animals of the World Series including *Elephants* by E. Rogers; *Lions* by M. M. Chipperfield; *Penguins* by R. Whitlock; *Zebras* by D. M. Goodall; *Chimpanzees* by R. Whitlock; *Kangaroos* by B. Stonehouse, and other titles.

Among the other titles published by Wayland are *Life in the Hedgerow*; *Life in the Meadow; Life on a Leaf; Life Around the Apple Tree*; *Life Among the Nettles*; *The Hollow Tree*.

The Human Body

Publisher: Burke Publishing Company Limited, Pegasus House, 116–20 Golden Lane, London EC1Y 0TL.

The *Do You Know About* Series including *Skin*; *Feet*; *Hair*; *Eyes*.

The Human Body by J. Howard, published by Macdonald Educational.

The Body Machine by C. Josephs, published by NCLS Limited, London.

Stomach and Intestines by Tage Voss, published by Angus and Robertson, London.

Hobbies

Let's Play Cards by J. Belton and J. Cramblit, published by Macdonald Educational, London.

Card Games and Tricks by P. Page, published by Macdonald Educational, London.

Party Games by D. Tibbit and D. Underwood, published by Ladybird Books, Loughborough.

Chess for Children by W. Lombardy and B. Marshall, published by Little, Brown and Company, Boston, USA.

I am a Ballerina by D. Swayne, published by J. M. Dent, London.

Junior Gymnastics by P. Aykroyd, published by Macdonald Educational, London.

Volleyball is for Me by A. Thomas, published by Lerner

Publications Co, Minneapolis, USA (published in Canada by J. M. Dent).

Track is for Me by A. L. Dickmeyer, published by Lerner Publications Co, Minneapolis, USA.

The Young Golfer by A. Hay and B. Robertson, published by Angus and Robertson, London.

A Day with a Footballer by A. Haddrell and C. Haddrell, published by Wayland, Hove, Sussex.

Your First Book of Tennis by J. Couvercelle and P. Lorin, published by Angus and Robertson, London.

The Outdoor Handbook published by Hamlyn, Feltham, Middlesex.

The following books from Pelham Books, London:

Badminton by P. Whetnall and S. Whetnall.

Squash Rackets by R. Hawkey.

Soccer by B. Wilson.

Cricket by B. Richards.

Table Tennis by C. Barnes.

Geography

Publisher: Hutchinson Books Limited, 17–21 Conway Street, London W1P 6JD.

The *Come To* Series including *France*; *USA*; *Russia*.

Publisher: Franklin Watts Limited, 12A Golden Square, London W1R 4BA.

The *Let's Go To* Series including *Spain*; *Japan*.

Publisher: A. & C. Black Publishers Limited, 35 Bedford Row, London WC1R 4JH.

Looking at Other Countries Series including *Norway*; *China*.

Beans Series including *Boy in Bangladesh*; *Arab Village*.

Publisher: Hamish Hamilton Limited, 57–9 Long Acre, London WC2E 9JZ.

Small World Series including *Eskimos*; *Whales*.

Publisher: Macdonald Educational, Maxwell House, 74 Worship Lane, London EC2A 2EN.

The *People's* Series including *Zulus*; *Amazon Indians*.

The *Countries* Series.

History

Picture Reference Books from Brockhampton Press (Hodder and Stoughton Children's Books, Sevenoaks, Kent TN13 2YA).

Looking at History Series by R. J. Unstead, published by A. & C. Black, London.

Growing Up in the Middle Ages by P. Davies, published by Wayland, Hove, Sussex.

Castles by D. Macaulay, published by Collins, London.

Illustrated History Books by G. Gyrille, published by Hart-Davis, London.

The Story of an English Village by J. Goodall, published by Macmillan, London.

Norman Britain by H. Loyn, published by Lutterworth Press, Guildford, Surrey.

How We Used to Live and *Peoples of the Past* – two series published by Macdonald Educational, London.

General interest

Publisher: Wayland Publishers Limited, 49 Lansdowne Place, Hove, Sussex BN3 1HF.

A Day With An Series including: *Airline Pilot*; *Ambulanceman*; *Doctor*; *Farmer*; *Fisherman*; *Lorry Driver*; *Miner*; *Nurse*; *Policeman*; *Shopkeeper*; *Vet*; *Vicar*.

Publisher: Macdonald Publishers Limited, Maxwell House, 74 Worship Street, London EC2A 2EN.

The *Insiders* Series including: *Airport*; *Department Store*; *Hospital*; *Hotel*; *Newspaper*; *Oil Rig*; *TV Studio*.

Publisher: Macmillan Publishers Limited, 4 Little Essex Street, London WC2R 3LF.

Look It Up Series including: *Sport and Entertainment*; *What People Do*; *World of Machines*.

Publisher: A. & C. Black Publishers Limited, 35 Bedford Row, London WC1R 4JH.

The A. and C. Black Junior Reference Books including: *Coal Mining*; *Fish and the Sea*; *Musical Instruments*.

What Makes It Go by J. Kaufman, published by Hamlyn, Feltham, Middlesex.

Religious Education

Publisher: Ladybird Books Limited, PO Box 12, Beeches Road, Loughborough LE11 2NQ.
The *Bible Books* Series including: *In the Beginning*; *Safe in the Ark*; *Jesus the Child*; *The Easter Story*.
The Life of Jesus by J. Robertson.

Publisher: Hodder and Stoughton Limited, Dunton Green, Sevenoaks, Kent TN13 2YA.
The *Bible Albums* Series including: *Jesus in His Early Years*; *In the Steps of Jesus*; *Jesus the Messiah*; *Jesus and the Pharisees*; *The First Easter*.

Chapter Twenty-nine

THE PROVISION OF SUPPORT FOR PARENTS

The knowledge that one has a handicapped child can be traumatic. There is a terrible sense of utter helplessness. There may be deep and unwarranted feelings of guilt. A family that can be encouraged to regard this as one of the greatest challenges they will ever have to meet, is well on the way to success. A family that can be encouraged to work together, to support each other, to delight in every small achievement will bring triumph out of disaster.

Life with a handicapped child is hard. For the mother there is not one hour when she can feel free from the burden of responsibility for the development of that child, unless she knows that there are others who are willing to shoulder the burden with her, and that the professional worker fully appreciates the depth of her problems and the urgency of her need.

WAYS IN WHICH THE PROFESSIONAL WORKER CAN HELP

The importance of early diagnosis

It is doubtful if this fact can ever be stressed sufficiently. In our own case we were incredibly lucky in the speed with which our suspicions were confirmed, and acted upon; in a specialist who was not afraid to tell the truth. The intuition of parents is often correct. Why is it that 20 years later there are still children who are allowed to slip through the net, that there are still parents who are left in a state of uncertainty and who therefore drift from one source of possible help to another. 'Don't worry. Come back in six months. He'll talk when he's ready' is the death-knell to the education of any deaf child.

Months, years, may be wasted in this way. It is vital that the education of the deaf child should begin at the earliest possible moment. It is too late to start at the age of three or four. Language and speech development should be underway long before that; vital stages can never be fully caught up.

The attitude of those providing diagnosis

The medical profession frequently has the unenviable task of imparting unwelcome information. While sympathising with this, I do not believe that the answer lies in a withdrawal technique. Parents who are confronted by the distressing knowledge that their baby is handicapped are in a state of shock. Understanding, realisation of what this means to them, even a little kindness, would go a long way towards dispelling some of that shock. They are not in a position to absorb technical details, they do not want to be blinded with science, they cannot take it in. A simple, caring explanation of what the handicap is, and of what it implies, are all that is necessary at this stage. A specialist who can be kind and yet firm, so that there is no room for doubt, is doing more for that child than he can possibly imagine. One who can impart a little encouragement is doing even more.

PARENTAL SUPPORT

I would like, from my own experience, to note the following points:

1. Parental support must begin at once – within days of diagnosis.
2. It must be consistent – at least fortnightly and at a regular time – and preferably when the professional worker can claim the mother's whole attention.
3. Those providing it must have a caring attitude. They must be prepared to listen to parents, to encourage them to talk out any feelings of guilt, of inadequacy, of isolation. They must work towards *acceptance* of the handicap.
4. Acceptance will be achieved more readily by action; the parent needs things to *do*; he needs to see results, however small these are.
5. The advice given must be clear and not muddled, firm and

not apathetic. The emphasis should be on the 'now' and not on the future.

6. It must be given with a sense of urgency – time is all-important – but never rushed and incomprehensible.

7. Parents are individuals. Some are extrovert enough to work with their child in front of another individual. Some may wish simply to watch and put the ideas into practice on their own.

8. The fact that this is a '*child*' first and foremost must be stressed. Discipline is important; a non-spoiling attitude is important. If the handicapped child is treated as a 'special case' in a social sense, there will be endless future problems not only for the child itself but also among the siblings.

9. Queries should be answered honestly. Other professional workers should be brought in whenever their help is needed. A deaf child imposes an enormous amount of strain in many directions.

10. Ideally extra visits should be paid when other members of the family, apart from the mother, are at home, so that all may feel involved in the development of this child and the strain on the mother may be lessened.

11. The mother should be encouraged to keep short notes of exactly what she has done with the child, and any progress that has been made. At first progress will be very, very slow and there will be periods when the child seems to have regressed, but it is encouraging to look back after a number of months and to see in black and white that progress has indeed been achieved.

12. The usefulness of a hearing aid and the importance of wearing it at all times must be stressed.

13. The difficulties pertaining to lip-reading must be pointed out and the best techniques explained.

14. Finally the mother must at all times have her confidence reinforced. She should never feel that the task is beyond her, that she needs to be clever in order to do it. It is demanding, yes, extremely so, but the instinctive love and sense of caring she feels towards that child should carry her through.

Only when the right sort of help is given early enough will our deaf children be given the chance to realise their full potential.

Chapter Thirty

THE HEARING IMPAIRED CHILD IN MAINSTREAM EDUCATION

It is not the intention of this book to delve deeply into how a severely deaf child may be successfully integrated into mainstream education. The subject is too broad in scope. The following notes, however, may be of interest to teachers in normal schools:

HOW CAN ONE PICK OUT A CHILD WITH DEFECTIVE HEARING?

1. Watch out for the child who stares too intently at your face. Perhaps he has become dependent upon lip-reading and is resourceful enough to make the best use of his eyes.
2. Do not be deceived by a child who nods his agreement each time you ask him if he has understood. The deaf are adept at this; they wish only to please you.
3. Watch out for the child who is inattentive. He could be deaf and unable to follow what you say.
4. Watch out for the child who is always seeking your attention. Is it because he is unable to follow general instructions?
5. Is there a child with certain speech difficulties? Does he pronounce consonants in a peculiar way? Does he omit the endings of words?
6. Is he unduly silent? Does he seldom contribute?
7. Is he exceptionally fidgety and quarrelsome? Perhaps he is frustrated at not understanding.
8. Does he frequently ask you to repeat things? Does he often look puzzled or surprised?
9. Is he always turning to his neighbour for help? Does he

watch his neighbour intently and then copy? If he is intelligent, he will find his own ways of coping with deafness.

10. Does he always turn his head sideways as you speak? Perhaps he is only hearing with one ear.

11. Is he quick at number work but surprisingly poor linguistically? Deaf children find language work much more difficult.

12. Does his voice seem too loud or too soft? Perhaps he cannot hear it well enough to modulate it.

Obviously there may be other reasons than deafness for many of the above. Nevertheless, deafness *could* be the cause, and it is well worth checking. A child suspected of being deaf should be tested at the earliest possible moment, in order that a hearing aid may be prescribed as soon as possible.

HOW TO HELP A HEARING IMPAIRED CHILD IN THE CLASSROOM

1. Are you aware of the most favourable conditions for lip-reading? (See Chapter 24.)

2. Is he sitting in the best possible place, i.e. near enough to you, but able to turn and see his classmates when they contribute to discussions?

3. Is his better ear towards you?

4. Is he getting the best possible use from his hearing aid? Does he: wear it every day?
   always have it switched on?
   change the batteries twice a week?
   ensure the leads are secure?
   keep the moulds free from wax?
   get it checked regularly?

5. Can you face him as much as possible and avoid at all costs 'talking to the blackboard'?

6. Can you enlist the sympathy of the other children so that they understand his problems and really want to help?

7. Can you seat him next to a child who is an extrovert; one who will be far more likely to help by explaining about games, outings, homework, etc. than an introverted child?

8. Can you cut down the amount of noise within the classroom? The more reverberation there is, the less intelligible will be your speech.

9. Can you establish a good rapport with the home, so that the necessary support is forthcoming?

10. Can you try to speak clearly, giving information precisely and instructions explicitly?

11. Can you summarise and reformulate what the other pupils have said so that he keeps abreast of discussions?

12. Can you supplement oral information with written information wherever possible?

13. Can you avoid talking to the pupils while their heads are down consulting diagrams or maps, or searching for information?

14. Can you give instructions in games, cookery, art, woodwork, etc. before the pupils' eyes go down to the task in hand?

15. If he is paired with another pupil for a project of some kind, can you again ensure that his partner is both an extrovert and a clear speaker?

16. Can you make time to test his understanding of lessons with detailed and searching questions?

17. And finally, can you achieve all of the above, without making either him or the class feel that he is too demanding of your time and attention? Too much attention will obviously be resented by the rest of the class; the intellectual gain may be defeated by the social loss.

Hearing impairment creates particular and unusual difficulties. They are not immediately obvious, and great sensitivity is demanded of the teacher. It is essential that adequate support should be available for every teacher who undertakes to accept hearing impaired pupils into his or her class.

Chapter Thirty-one

CHILDREN OF ANOTHER WAY

This book has been concerned throughout with those whose problem is simply deafness, with their integration into the normal hearing world, and with the statement that with determination on the one side, and understanding on the other, such integration is both possible and desirable.

It is not within the scope of this book to discuss those who have a double handicap, who are not only deaf, but blind, or deaf and brain damaged, or deaf and unable to lip-read, or deaf with a different mother-tongue. To omit the discussion of these problems is in no way to fail to recognise them or to minimise them. They are immense, but they are different. Unfortunately in the mind of the general public they have become analogous. The public hears much, and rightly so, about the wonderful ways in which blind and brain-damaged deaf children can be helped into learning by the use of signs. The public hears very little about the struggle of the more numerous group – those born simply deaf – towards normality.

I believe that children who have no other problem but deafness, can and should be integrated into the hearing world, and that their greatest happiness and fulfilment lie in achieving this. But I acknowledge that in some situations such integration may be neither possible nor desirable. Any child needs to feel thoroughly accepted within his home environment. If that environment is one where signing is the norm, because both parents are deaf then it is only natural that he should learn to sign. To feel at home within his family is of more importance psychologically than to embark upon the endless struggle of learning to speak.

Similarly, a child who is multiply-handicapped, especially if the secondary handicap be brain-damage, may well have the greatest difficulty in learning to lip-read and may well need the support of manualism. Similarly with a child who is both blind and deaf, but here a great deal depends upon the severity of each handicap. I have known children categorised as deaf-blind who have learnt to speak most successfully; neither handicap is usually total.

The child with a different mother-tongue, presents again a most difficult problem. How can one provide the repetition and reinforcement of language so sorely needed by all those born deaf, if the language used at home is different from the language used at school? Does the answer lie in manualism, or does it not? Adequate solutions have yet to be found; much discussion has yet to take place.

For all these children it may indeed be necessary to provide another way. It is the birthright of every child to achieve his full potential.

USEFUL ORGANISATIONS

The Royal National Institute for the Deaf
105 Gower Street
London WC1E 6AH   01–387 8033

National Deaf Children's Society
45 Hereford Road
London W2 5AH   01–229 9272

Beethoven Fund for Deaf Children
2 Queensmead, St Johns Wood Park
London NW8 6RE   01–586 8107

Breakthrough Trust
Charles Gillett Centre, Selly Oak Colleges
Birmingham B29 6IE   021–472 6448 (voice)
                                            021–471 1001 (DCT)

British Association of the Hard of Hearing
7/11 Armstrong Road
London W3 7JL   01–743 1110

British Deaf Association
38 Victoria Place
Carlisle CA1 1HU   0228 48844

National Bureau for Handicapped Students
40 Brunswick Square
London WC1N 1AZ   01–278 3459

National Children's Bureau
8 Wakly Street, Islington
London EC1V 7QE   01–278 9441

Voluntary Council for Handicapped Children
8 Wakly Street, Islington
London EC1V 7QE   01–278 9441

National Council of Social Workers with the Deaf
c/o Social Services Department
17–23 Clements Road, Ilford
Essex IG1 1BL   01–478 3020 ext 58

British Association of Teachers of the Deaf
The Rycroft Centre, Stanley Road
Cheadle Hulme, Cheshire SK8 6RF   061–437 5951

National Study Group on Further and Higher Education
    for the Hearing Impaired
Bournville College of Further Education
Bristol Road South, Northfield
Birmingham B31 2AJ

Play Matters (The Toy Libraries Association)
Seabrook House, Wyllyotts Manor
Darkes Lane, Potters Bar EN6 2HL   Potters Bar 44571

Scottish Association for the Deaf
Moray House, Holyrood Road
Edinburgh EH8 8AQ   031–556 8455

UNITED STATES OF AMERICA

John Tracy Clinic
806 West Adams Boulevard
Los Angeles, California 90006

Alexander Graham Bell Association for the Deaf (AGBAD)
3417 Volta Place NW
Washington DC 20007

Oral Deaf Adults Section
address as for AGBAD above

International Parents' Organization
c/o AGBAD (address above)

American Deafness and Rehabilitation Association
814 Thayer Avenue
Silver Spring, Maryland 20910

Council on Education of the Deaf
c/o John Tracy Clinic (address above)

National Association of the Deaf
814 Thayer Avenue
Silver Spring, Maryland 20910

National Foundation for Children's Hearing Education and
Research (Deaf)
928 McLean Avenue
Yonkers, NY 10704

Hear Center (Deaf)
301 E Del Mar Boulevard
Pasadena, California 91101

International Association of Parents of the Deaf
814 Thayer Avenue
Silver Spring, Maryland 20910

AUSTRALIA

Australian Deafness Council
PO Box 60, Curtin
Australian Capital Territories 2605

Better Hearing Australia
5 High Street
Victoria 3181

Federation of Adult Deaf Societies
c/o Wellington Parade
East Melbourne, Victoria 3002

Visiting Teacher Service for Deaf Children
PO Box 250, Ferntree Gully
Victoria 3156

Note: All State education departments are responsible for the
education of deaf children and should be contacted in the state
concerned.